THE HEART IN THE CASKET

Sometimes Cathleen came close to hoping Rosamund would go. For even now, how unpredictably and woundingly her temper blazed. How like her ruthless father she was as she stood all akimbo, granite-faced, with eyes of ultimate ice-blue . . . What she really needs, Cathleen thought again, is a lover . . .

"You're a bully!" said Cathleen. "I don't like bullies." For once she didn't offer to retract. "I love you very much, Rosamund, but I hate that cruel streak in you."

"Well that's the way I am," said her daughter . . . "There's something about you that gets me, though. You ask to be hurt." And she was gone.

THE HEART
IN THE CASKET

Colleen Klein

ARROW BOOKS

Arrow Books Limited
62–65 Chandos Place, London WC2N 4NW

An imprint of Century Hutchinson Limited

London Melbourne Sydney Auckland
Johannesburg and agencies throughout
the world

First published in Great Britain
by Century Hutchinson 1985

Arrow edition 1986

© Colleen Klein 1977

None of the characters in this fable is in any way
based upon any human being living, dead, or moribund

Printed and bound in Great Britain by
Anchor Brendon Limited, Tiptree, Essex

ISBN 0 09 949620 8

TO MY MOTHER

1

"Rosamund?" said the young girl, tentatively. She tried it again, this time more firmly. "Rosamund. Do you like that name?" She looked down at the thatch of black hair, so different from her own, and folded the crib-blanket back from the minute face. "Rosamund Bell."

In the lonely months of waiting and marking time and curbing her tongue she had fallen into the habit of talking to herself; silently, for the most part, but once in a while she heard herself saying a word or a phrase or even a sentence aloud. Oh, but now she would no longer be alone! There would always be someone to talk to, always someone to listen; best of all, someone to answer.

The crumpled rose of the baby's face gave no sign of liking the name she would respond to in the years to come. As to whether it would suit her, who could tell? All that Cathleen knew was that it had sprung unbidden to her mind, and there was no way she could change it now.

The flurry at the door heralded the coming of the nurse, avid for a morsel of chatter while she kidnapped the babies from their mothers, and straightened the beds for the visitors to come.

She paused at Cathleen's bed. "She looks like you."

Cathleen smiled back. "Oh, I don't think so. Her eyes are blue and her hair's black."

"That doesn't mean a thing. The eyes'll change colour, probably, they often do, and the first hair mostly falls out anyway. You see, she'll end up with brown eyes and brown hair like her mum, won't you lovie? Come on, Mrs. Bell, finish burping her and hand her over."

Who is Mrs. Bell, Cathleen wondered, before she remembered. For she, too, had taken on a new identity; Cathleen McKinnon was Cathleen Bell, married woman. Or so the fiction went. In fact she had searched the pages of the telephone book for a name anonymous without being commonplace, one with a ring to it; and, literally, that was what she found. Cathleen Bell is a no-name; protective cover, she thought again. But

Rosamund Bell sounds like roses and fountains splashing and birds calling.

"Do you like the name Rosamund?" she asked. "Rose of the world, that's what it means."

"I like it alright," said the porky little nurse, wrinkling up her freckled schoolgirl face. She was not long out of school, either, probably Cathleen's own age, eighteen or so. "But listen, what about all the super ones in the baby book I lent you?"

Cathleen McKinnon had been taught by her parents, by word and by example, to be polite. She had accepted the book, food-stained from many mealtime scrutinies, with thanks, and pretended to pore over the pages, while in her bones she had felt that the perfect name would come to her of its own volition, rise unbidden from her stream of being (as indeed it had) and that she would know it at once, by heart.

"What's her daddy called?" asked the nurse, taking the moist bundle from Cathleen's arms.

Cathleen hesitated. She had grown reticent these last months. Unused to lying, shy and reserved by nature, she had come to use the armour of silence to guard her secrets. "It was Brian," she said, after a moment, judging that the truth would give nothing away.

"What about Bryony, then? That's a nice unusual name, you don't hear it every day. We had a really gorgeous little red-headed baby in last month, oh well actually she was in a private ward. Rich!—you never saw such presents. First grandchild on both sides! Her daddy was Brian too, so they settled on Bryony. Flowers!—I never saw so many flowers in my—" Her eyes rested on the empty vase by Cathleen's bed, and she faltered. "Better get going," she muttered, and turned towards the other beds.

My baby will be poor, thought Cathleen. But I'll love her for a hundred rich relations, and she'll be beautiful and good and clever, please God. How lucky I am—she looked with great pity at the girl in the bed next to her, the girl whose baby had died, who lay in a drugged sleep, with tearstains on her cheeks, waiting for her milk to be dried up, so that she could go home to nothing. Her third still-born child, the nurse had said, and she had nearly died too. They had fixed it, the doctors, so that she would never have another child. Poor thing, she might as well have died, thought Cathleen, and involuntarily she pressed her hands to her own round breasts. Her body, familiar for so long, was strange to her, was passing strange, in fact was wondrous, she thought, misquoting on purpose. Shakespeare always has a word for it. And she blessed again her father who had bored her to tears as a child, imprisoning her while he read Shakespeare aloud; easing his own heart's sadness with the poetry that reminded him that all men were born to suffer, that he had not been singled out. How she had hated it! Loving him utterly, she had still longed to have a jolly father who played golf and read the newspapers, as the other girls' did.

And now—years later—buffeted by fortune as he had been—she found comfort, as he had done, in words that went straight to her heart, reminding her that lost love is an old story as well as a new one, that girls betrayed and abandoned make a long roll-call. Girls have always been lovers and losers. The name of the game is love, and if you play it, you abide by the rules.

It was visiting time. She put away her father's Shakespeare, the red leather cover dulled and rubbed thin by his hands. Instead, she pretended absorption in a magazine, garish and tinny, which the nurse had lent her. Soon some visitor down the aisle would come to borrow her bedside chair, it was always a race to see which of the other six patients got in first. They had caught on quickly to the fact that she had no visitors at all; women are always clued-up. Yes, now; a pleasant voice asked whether she could spare it—*spare* it—and she lifted her eyes briefly and nodded assent. Soon the hour would be over, they would scrape back their chairs and call their goodbyes; and it would be mothers and babies only, all on the same footing again. Except for the sad girl in the next bed, cracking hardy, flanked by a bevy of relatives also cracking hardy. So what am I whingeing about, thought Cathleen; there's always someone worse off.

The bell did go. The ward emptied, and the fat young nurse came back to collect the vases of flowers. She stood at the end of Cathleen's bed and shifted her weight from one stocky leg to the other.

"Look, I don't know how you're placed, Mrs. Bell," she said, all in a rush. "But I reckon you're up against it. So tell me to shut up if you like, but if you're interested, I reckon I can get

9

you a job with my auntie down in Sydney. Great-auntie she is really, a real good sort, not that I see much of her these days. She's a sort of an invalid, but not bed-ridden, if you know what I mean, just wonky in the legs and all that. She needs someone to stay with her and keep the house clean and keep her company. The last old girl she had took to the bottle, and she swears she won't have any one else there ever again. But my mum reckons she's lonely, so if you like I'll write to her about you and the baby. Mind you, she won't pay you anything, just food and board, she's only got her pension really, but the house is right near the water, near a little park. It's on the bay, it's a lovely spot." She stopped, her voice had grown louder as she went along, and she flushed as she caught the rivetted eyes of the other women, mouse-still as women are when they are trying to find out something, and conscious that the smallest movement might interrupt the flow.

"She'll be nice to the baby," she went on, more softly. "She loves babies, she never had one herself." In a voice even softer, muffled by embarrassment, she added, "Well, it was just an idea. I didn't mean to offend you."

"Offend me?" cried Cathleen, daring at last to breathe. "Oh I could kiss your feet!"

"Don't do that, for crikey's sake," said the nurse, relaxing into laughter. "After a day in this joint they stink!"

Cathleen laughed aloud for joy. Nice to the baby! A house near the bay! Oh bliss! "My cup runneth over," she said.

"Hey!" shouted the nurse. "Don't you dare! Not before I bring your bed pan!"

All the women burst out laughing. They all laughed, members of a secret society, conspirators for the moment, not competing, citizens of a manless world.

"Who's got stitches?" whooped the nurse, red-faced, still chuckling. "I'll wash you down now, girls, before I do the flowers. —Oh, if my mum could only see me now, washing bums for a living!" She turned to go, presenting her solid white backside to them, a country girl, sturdy and kind, hamming it up a little, playing to the gallery, doing a Chaplin shuffle out of the room.

2

So here she was back in Sydney, Cathleen Bell, ensconced with her child in a tumbledown house in a weed-cluttered garden by the bay, custodian of an auntie called Mrs. Llewellyn, a vast old lady with the face of a witch and the heart of a fairy godmother. Cathleen was busy, and she was grateful; therefore she was happy.

More and more, silence became second nature to her; the less she spoke the less likely it was that her secrets would be discovered. Here in Alcheringa, Cathleen Bell, young mother, young widow (as she presented herself) was a world away from Cathleen McKinnon, only child, and child only. She girded herself now for her own child's sake, as she had once girded herself for her mother, and found within herself reserves of strength and endurance that surprised her. She had never been a chatterer; to think and to listen, to say only what she meant, had been her mode of expression and her role in life. The words that swarmed thick in the beehive of her mind did not come easily to her tongue; she had been brought up in a quiet house, where the only echoing words, the only resonances, were those penned by an Elizabethan poet three hundred, four hundred years before. Her parents, never gabby, had grown quieter as the years went on.

And so Brian had enthralled her more utterly; captured her with his Irish tongue as much as with the Irish blue of his eyes. With his words that spilled and leaped like quicksilver, with his moods and caprices that seemed so remote and charming to her own unswerving nature, he was a creature from another world: the world of dream. It had seemed to her fantastic that he had chosen to love her. She was shattered but not amazed when after three months he chose to leave her.

From the start, from the first meeting of their eyes at the playhouse she had felt she was too staid for him. From that first ill-fated moment, she had admired him too openly—but what was she to do? She had never learned to dissemble. Loved, but not cossetted, brought up to do her duty, the only child of parents born middle-aged, she had never thought of herself as possessing any measure of charm. The boys who asked her to

11

play tennis were cast in her own mould; sensible lads destined for a stint in the public service, or perhaps, pinnacle of pinnacles, a career in medicine or law. They had no thought of committing themselves, any more than she had; life moved in orderly progressions, one safe step after the other.

And all of a sudden, between sunrise and sunset, it seemed, everything was changed. Her father, unbelievably, was dead. The war wounds that took him to hospital from time to time, this time took him for good and all. Those wounds of body and spirit that he brought from the Burma railway, that had turned him, always tall, always pallid, into a wraith, still loving but querulous, wary, anxious—now they had severed them. Anguished, brought face to face with anguish at sixteen, she had stood by his coffin; despairing, she had looked up to see her own despair mirrored in her mother's eyes. He was forty-three. There was nothing much he had to leave them. To Cathleen's mother went the photographs of a thin laughing young man in a round-necked bathing-costume, together with a pile of fading letters, and a gramophone with a stack of well-played records; and the meagre insurance policy. To Cathleen went his Shakespeare, the one from which he had read the plays to her as a child, the one he had left her when he went to war, in case, as he said, he never came back. And one other heritage; her mother.

"Look after your mother, Cathleen, when I die," he had said as if in jest. "She can't look after herself."

So Cathleen did. For the two years her mother's life stretched out, thinning day by day, while Cathleen trained to teach little children, and came home dutifully cheerful to a cheerless house, she kept her promise to her father. She saw her mother grow more frail and wan each week, watched her pine away from grief. Cancer, they said it was; cancer of the breast that had invaded her whole system. If only she had come to the doctors sooner—but Cathleen wondered.

Two years later to the day, to the very day of her father's death, she stood beside her dead mother, so thin, so painfully thin, so waxen-pale, like an old-woman doll, her face ancient yet unmarked by life, as if she had never lived at all. With eyes that ached from tears unshed, with a throat that rasped from sobs unuttered, she stood, gathering herself to go on with a life

12

that seemed pointless. She was the apple of their eyes; and they were dead.

Alone, except for a knot of neighbours, she stood by the graveside in the rain, and dry-eyed watched the rivulets run down the mound of red clay. So this was the end of all loving.

Her father's daughter, facing each day as he had faced each hopeless day in Burma, she forced herself to cope with the sad duties imposed by sudden death. Her mother's daughter, calm despite the grief and pain that filled her, she kept a composed face as she went to her lectures and practised her teaching skills. The spring that came bursting through the warm earth, the jasmine and wisteria seemed a travesty. At eighteen, she saw each azure day as grey, or livid.

"Will they send us to the country?" the girls at college asked, pretending to shiver. They were a year or two older than Cathleen, for the most part; she had been the youngest girl in her class, and the brightest. It was only her father's death that had stopped her from taking a university scholarship.

"Cathleen, do you care if you get sent to Woop-Woop?" someone asked.

Cathleen shrugged; she hardly cared. The house they had rented for years was let to others now, and she lived at a hostel, surrounded by other girls, but still alone. People were kind to her at first, then shunned her; misery is catching.

And then, radiantly, he came. Like Jove descending. Why his gaze lighted on her she did not know—or at least not then. For every brilliant peacock there is a dun-coloured pea-hen, the duller the background the more he flaunts his plumage, she thought wryly as time went on. But at first meeting she was dazzled, dizzy at her miraculous good fortune. Later, months later, wounded and puzzled, striving against embitterment, she thought that the reason for his choice was simple and cynical; she lacked protectors.

She felt his eyes on her, while the young amateurs on stage ranged their way through Pygmalion. He was sitting next to her, alone, as she was. Her friend Barbara was up on stage, making an ass of herself as Professor Higgins' mother, flourishing a lorgnette.

Conscious of his gaze, she still somehow managed to watch the stage. Something in the way that Barbara sent her words

13

winging towards him made Cathleen realize that this man was
the one who haunted Barbara's dreams, the painter she spoke of
as a genius. Sitting quite still, as was her custom, Cathleen
racked her brains to remember what else Barbara had said
of him. Brian—what—Gogarty—Fogarty—Gehogan—some
name like that—A Bohemian, a genius, a rebel—But then
Barbara had always been fulsome about the people she chose to
admire, and more often than not, her swans were geese. She and
Cathleen had been friends for years, and she alone had stayed a
true friend when their shared school days were done, and their
paths diverged.

And that is how I repaid her, thought Cathleen, by thieving
the fellow she was in love with—although in the end it was a
good turn I did her. Or bad, she amended, hugging the baby in
her arms—And the road I set foot on that night in November,
that languorous and balmy night, has brought me here to
dreamtime. So much had happened in the year. One year.

She was sitting in the westering sunshine, in an old cane
chair. The old lady who lived in the old house (everything here
was tottering to its end) was disposed for her afternoon snooze.
Cathleen's baby, a warm wet bundle in a flannelette rug lay in
her arms, as replete as a boa-constrictor. I really ought to moo,
thought Cathleen, I am like a fat brown cow, feeding my baby
and ruminating in the sun. Once I was slender, now I am thick,
my belly is marked, no doubt for life, and I don't care at all.
What mattered was the child in her arms, the roof over her
head, the flowering plot of earth, the sound-hearted sweet old
crone who had given them shelter.

"Rosamund," crooned Cathleen rubbing the baby's back as
the old lady, Mrs. Llewellyn had taught her to do. The baby
burped—belched, really—and smiled, gazing at her mother
with eyes of the most vivid and tender blue. Her father's eyes.

Cathleen bit back tears; no use to long for him, he had gone
his ways. Thou'lt come no more, never, never, never, never,
never! She had tried to hate him; useless. Now she must learn to
forget him. But when she looked at the exquisite miniature of
his face, she felt again the helpless acquiescence of that first
moment.

For from the first moment that he had fallen into step with
her in the city street, accommodating his long stride to hers, she

14

had been ready to follow him through all the streets of the world, if he beckoned her.

What he asked of her was less; only that she should share his bed. As one in a trance she had followed him to his squalid narrow room in a dirty street in Darlinghurst. She closed her eyes now, not at the glare of sunshine, but at the sudden glare of memory. Unversed and innocent though she was, she was no stranger in this unknown country; it seemed that she knew it all at first sight, that each step, so tentative and yet so sure, was one that she had taken before, that she had been born to take. Hungry to live again, innocent and sensual, she had held out her arms to him and laughed aloud for joy.

"I don't know whether you're one of the wise or foolish virgins," he murmured, leaning on his elbow, and smiling down at her—"But if I'd known, Kate, I'd never have presumed to make a pass. Lovely Kate—"

"I'm very glad you did," she answered primly. That made them both laugh. He kissed her again, then he got up and dressed and went out for hamburgers. She hugged her knees against her chest, and smiled to herself and counted the minutes until he came back.

"I was lucky," said Cathleen, to the gurgling baby with her father's eyes, "Even if it only lasted for a minute."

A minute it had seemed, no more. Three months, four months, can they pass in a minute? They did. She did as he bade her. She left the hostel without a backward glance, without regret, without even a forwarding address. The term was over. When the long blue official letter came with the notice of her teaching appointment, she was camping with him out in the summer bushland, under the stars. While he sketched the strange shapes of dead trees and anthills, she watched his big hands and beaky Irish nose, and adored him.

"I'm your lubra, Brian," she told him, as she gathered twigs to boil the billy.

"Come here and kiss me, lubra," he ordered, still painting, putting his left arm out to gather her close.

How happy we were! How poor, how rich! I worked as a waitress at the seedy café in Orange, he painted a mural for it, with orange wheat and kookaburras on blackened trees; we ate for a month on what we earned there, we lived like spendthrifts.

15

At night we made love, at daybreak, at noontide. Our skins ran rivers of sweat, and we swam ourselves clean in the billabong. Only last year. Only last summer.

How moody he was, how impatient, how suddenly his temper flared!

"Don't be so stupid, Cathleen! Don't be so hidebound!" He was furious because she had demurred about swimming naked. "Who's going to spy on you? The kookaburras? Suburban miss! Middle-class morality!" he mocked her.

So she tore off her clothes, dived in. She swam much better than he did, faster and with more style. Swimming and playing the piano, Cathleen McKinnon was good at those.

"Come back. Naiad! Water nymph!" he called, chasing her, blowing out water like a whale spouting. "Cathleen, I'm drowning!" He feigned panic, and in four swift strokes she was beside him. He caught and kissed her, pulled her under. They came up spluttering and laughing. How lovely it was!

How soon it ended! In three months she was pregnant. She came to tell him one hot morning filled with the smell of gum leaves and harsh cawing as the crows flew over. Fearful but full of joy, with cast-down eyes she spoke to him. He heard her out, with a frozen face.

She faltered into silence, then met his eyes. "But you're pleased, Brian? You don't mind. Do you?"

"*Pleased*! You fool!" he said, looking at her with such hatred that she recoiled. "How could I be pleased? I don't want a child. I have to be free! I always told you that I have to be free!"

"But—it won't make any difference."

"It will. It must. Look, Cathleen, I have to go to England next year. I can't afford a wife. You knew that."

"If I teach—" she said despairingly, forced to beg and barter, hating herself for it. "If we get married and I ask them to let me teach, I'll beg them—I can help you to save up. I won't be a burden—"

"I have to go alone." Savagely he kicked at a stone. "I'm only twenty-two. I can't afford to be tied down. And anyway—"

"Anyway what?"

"A bind like that means death to an artist."

Cathleen heard the finality in his voice, knew that he spoke what was truth for him. She was crying now. "I'll help you to

16

save the money, I told you. I won't even ask to go with you.—
But our baby—"

He hit her across the face, so hard that her head jerked back,
"Stupid! How stupid can you be! I can't be emotionally tied.
I've got to be free to explore myself."

She was shocked as much as wounded. Her own temper rose
to match his. They faced each other in hatred.

"You'll find a desert inside you. Heartless!" Their breathing
came in rasps as they glared at each other, enemies. "Be free,
then!" she sobbed, "Consider yourself free."

"You might be mistaken," he muttered after a moment. "You
can't be sure." When she shook her head he spoke with cold
finality. "Then the only thing to do is to have an abortion."

"No," said Cathleen. "Never!"

"You bitch!" he cried violently, his face contorted and ugly.
"You did it on purpose!" The strange Irish temper that flickered
always behind his eyes, flashed now in his murderous face, his
mouth thinned to a slash, his eyes greyed-over and sharp as
scimitars. "I ought to kill you!"

"Kill me then," whispered Cathleen. "I don't care!"

He turned in a jerk, went into the tent. He came back, still
moving like a puppet, and thrust a paper at her, and something
else—a wad of bank notes. Unbelievably. They both watched as
the money fluttered through her fingers to the ground.

"I was saving this for my trip. Here, take it. The address, it's a
nurse, Mick's cousin, she'll take care of you. She's quite reliable,
clean and—"

He stopped. Cathleen was screaming. She screamed for her
father dead, for her mother in the red sodden clay, for the love
smashed to pieces before her eyes. She screamed and then she
sobbed and at last she hiccupped into silence.

He picked up his money, and folded it before he tucked it
away. He was thinking. In a low voice he spoke, at last. "I'll
take you back to Orange, if I can get the car started. We can't go
on. Take the money to get you back to Sydney. Kate—I said
will you take the money to get you back home?"

Lies, all lies. He knew she had no home. She did not answer.

He tried again. "You can see it's no good, Cathleen. We can't
go on now. Cathleen—"

"Don't say any more." She stopped him with a thrust of

17

clenched fists. "Don't take me to the town. I'll make my own way. You're safe."

She turned and walked from him. She moved blindly from the camp by the billabong, the ashes of the fire, the beat-up car, and struck out towards the highway where some farmer, some traveller, anyone would take her somewhere, anywhere, away from her cruel-hearted lover.

He stood silent and watched her go and made no move to stop her.

Cathleen opened her eyes, screwed-up from the pain of remembering, and forced herself to step back to the present. That was the end of it all, she thought; the end of all loving is losing. Here endeth the third lesson, and the most bitter. My mother and father, they were my past—and he was my future. In her bones she knew that she would never see him again, or only at first remove, in his daughter's eyes. My daughter's, mine, not his, she amended furiously. And as long as I live he'll never set eyes on her. He had his chance, and he missed it. With a dawning cynicism that the months alone had taught her, she was certain that he, Narcissus incarnate, would adore the small face, set forever in his own image. As for me, I'd love her if she looked like an ape, or a leprechaun—or—Or even like you, Jumbo, she said to the ugly little mongrel dog at her feet. Grizzled and old he was, like everything else in this house; but loving, like old Mrs. Llewellyn.

I have come to a house of love, she thought, and her spirits lifted. And you and I, Rosamund, we are at the beginning of things, not at the end.

Each day Cathleen grew stronger. She washed and ironed, cleaned and dusted, listened to Mrs. Llewellyn's interminable sorties into her Victorian childhood, read aloud to her, learned to crochet, fell into bed so tired that sleep came swiftly, sweet and dreamless. She saw her baby grow, watching the little fingers learn to reach and grasp, the wobbly head grow stronger on its frail column of neck. The black hair fell out and was replaced by pale silk, yellow and straight as corn. Each day of her present was so happy that she despised herself for her recapitulation of the past, and yet she could not help herself.

All her girlhood days had followed the rules set down for her. She had moved from home to school to piano lesson to swimming baths, to Manly beach for a week's ecstatic holiday, sometimes. Two or three friends. No straying off course.

Lying out on the lawn, looking over to the bay while her two charges slept the sleep of the very young and the very old, Cathleen found herself going over and over the last year—not Brian, not the passages of love between them, which had proved him false—but the people she had met, the places where she stayed. Most of all, the kindness she had found in the most unlikely places.

Broke and broken, she had come to the Red Cross rooms to ask for food and shelter till she found work; and met with the most abundant spilling over of kindness. One lie she told them—did they know it was a lie?—that her husband had left her. Husband, not lover. The rest was true, that she was an orphan, that she had no relations in Australia. Poor child, they clucked, and did their best to comfort her with hot tea and home-made scones and clichés full of optimism and kindness. Every cloud has a silver lining, it's a long lane that has no turning, all of those. One of them, thin and elegant, more worldly than the rest, took her into a corner, and pressed a slip of paper into her hand.

"Ring me at home in the morning," she said. "Or come to see me, if you like. Before ten."

The room the Red Cross ladies procured for Cathleen at the People's Palace was much less than palatial. After a night of tears and tossing she was glad to come downstairs and put her pennies into the public telephone, warm and foetid though it was from the breath of the last user. Without much hope she pushed the button, and listened to the voice at the other end, and as she listened her hopes quickened.

"I really shouldn't be saying this, my dear," said the hollow voice in her ear, "But—well—something like this happened to me once. So if your husband—has disappointed you, why not change your name by deed-poll, I did. And you know what I'd do. I'd get work at one of the mental hospitals—psychiatric hospitals they call them now—they pay very well—just for a month or two. Save your money. Are you there? Can you hear me?"

"Yes, I can hear you."

19

"Save your money and go down to Melbourne or up to Brisbane and start all over again. Shed this life. That is if you have no one at all."

"No one," said Cathleen mournfully.

"And your baby will have a fresh start, too."

"I was going to be a teacher. But they wouldn't want me now.—I'm not married," said Cathleen.

"I thought perhaps you weren't. So get yourself a new name, for your baby's sake. Call in at the Red Cross rooms this afternoon—I'm not rostered, but I'll be there, about two or thereabouts. We won't speak of this again. I'd be tarred and feathered if anyone knew. But once—well, that's all past history—" She gave a sigh. "Are you there?—Yes, well I'll lend you the money to get you started. Don't thank me, child, just pass it on some day to another girl in a fix. It's a big boat and we're all in it together—What did you say?"

"Lovers and losers," said Cathleen.

With the photographic memory that had made school a breeze, Cathleen remembered the words, the hot sore ring around her ear as she replaced the receiver. She saw again the well-used, well-lived in face of the society matron in cream silk who slipped an envelope into her hand. It held twenty pounds, the same as Brian had offered. But it was life, not death she had to buy with this money, and she took it with great gratitude.

"So you've located some relatives?" said the woman, in her well-bred Point Piper voice, pitched a little higher than usual. "Oh, good show! Good luck then, my dear." On the way out Cathleen turned to look back; and the woman was staring after her like one who looked down a long corridor of years.

So Cathleen had gone. She found work again as a waitress, a hamburger joint by the quay, so dirty that the regulars called it the sty. She stayed on at the People's Palace. She applied for work at Callan Park, as a trainee nurse, and she was taken on. She hated it; she pitied the plight of the patients too much and only the need to protect herself stopped her from involving herself in their problems to the point of no recall. She had her own room there, clean and spare. The uniforms she chose were a size too big, for her waistline was slipping away and her

20

breasts, always rounded, were noticeably bigger. She felt very
well, her cheeks glowed pink beneath the tan she still had kept
as souvenir. A letter tied with blue, a photograph or two, I
count them all anew, among my souvenirs,—or some such
syrup, where had she heard it—on her father's gramophone
perhaps? Yes, that was it.

She listened to the chatter of the other nurses, and smiled,
and said nothing; she felt infinitely older and wiser. Boyfriends
they talked about, and getting the hard word put on you. They
seemed babes in the wood. She sat at the table with them and
felt her baby stir, a movement as fragile as a bubble, and she
rejoiced.

The patients liked her, she was sweet and gentle with them.
When her growing bulk made it apparent that she must move
on, she was sad to leave them; all the young kids struggling to
understand themselves, and the middle-aged and old who
would never get out of the morass. Their sad derangement
discomposed but did not shatter her; she had to protect herself.
She felt like a vessel laden with precious oils. I guess this is how
Mary felt about Jesus, she thought, well, she was a girl like me,
and she didn't ask to be chosen any more than I did. And if
that's blasphemy—and I suppose my mother would say it is—
then I can't help it. Quickly she thrust the thoughts of her
parents from her mind, the distress and horror they would feel
at her situation. Well, if they hadn't left me, she thought—not
that they could help it—if I hadn't been so alone it might have
been different.

When it was time to go, for her girth would soon not pass for
robustness, Cathleen had a hundred and nine pounds saved.
The hard work and the nourishing food, the hours of regular
sleep had steadied and strengthened her, till she looked like a
country wench, rosy and strapping.

So now she had a new persona as well as a new name.
Cathleen Bell. When she looked in her mirror, she hardly
recognised herself. She sat up all night in the train to Brisbane,
hoarding her money (sleepers come dear) for one thing, and too
excited to sleep for another. She had never been so far from
Sydney. Dark came down quickly, for it was midwinter, but she
stared out of the window at the lights of the towns, more strung
out as the train lurched further away from the city. It was the

old-fashioned train that had taken her, not the new streamlined one; the seats were tattered, and it rattled and groaned over the rails as if to make sure that the riders within would share its aching bones. Cathleen did not mind. She grew more excited as each small station they passed grew more tropical. She could not believe her eyes when she saw an orange bougainvillea—orange—tumbling over a lighted station building. Bougainvillea—in winter.

At Coff's Harbour the train stopped with a jerk. She slipped out of the carriage and stepped out on the platform into a world of trees like umbrellas and banana fronds and palms and red hibiscus. She smiled with delight. The young porter at the station stopped loading crates for a moment and grinned back at her.

"Pretty, isn't it love?" he said, very Strine, "You're in the tropics now."

She clasped her hands, squeezed them together with happiness. Light from the station lamp gleamed on her new wedding ring. She leaned back against the carriage door and watched the young porter. For the first time for months life seemed sweet again, and full of promise. Her baby—Oh she could hardly wait. Boy or girl, it didn't matter; it would be someone to love, someone who would love back, not offer love then snatch it away. She felt fulfilled; she had a future as well as a past. Life was sweet.

"Here, baby!" said the porter, young, handsome and cheeky. "Have a banana." He hung a great bunch of bananas over her arm, green as grass they were, beautiful. "They grow well up here. All I want's a kiss."

Cathleen burst out laughing at his comical cheeky Australian face, so ready to give anything a go.

"Okay," she said. In the quiet station, with nobody else abroad, she placed a light kiss on his cheek, then another on his lips.

"Hey, come back," he called, but she shook her head, cradled the swag of bananas in her arms, and closed the carriage door behind her. The train gave its macabre whistle, pitched between a hoot and a screech, and groaned into motion. Cathleen sat in the dark carriage, listened to the breathing and snoring of the other passengers, held the bananas against her belly, where, behind the wall of silky skin, her baby stirred in sleep. She smiled into the darkness.

3

And the years passed, in the village called Dreamtime, as quickly as a dream. The baby who had slept in Cathleen's arms could sit up, could crawl, could walk, could hold out arms, could prattle.

Seasons came and went. The bay that in summer was aquamarine, changed in winter to stormy grey. Sullen beneath the lowering skies it scowled anger at summer's forsaking. Winter winds pummelled the water, sheets of sudden rain blotted it out. Behind the streaming panes they watched, the three of them, child and crone, and the young woman in the middle; heard bells jangling on the moored boats.

And each year the winter that would never end, ended; and the spring that would never come, crept in. Time was telescoped for Cathleen. She tended her child, rejoicing in her beauty; tended the old woman, accepting an ugliness made tolerable by her kindness. They respected each other, which was a great help in the close quarters they shared. Cathleen took half a dozen pupils to learn to play on Mrs. Llewellyn's old upright piano, sunburned children longing to get back to the beach.

The two women were united in their adoration of the child. But when Mrs. Llewellyn's ancient friends came to see her, Cathleen and Rosamund made their escape for an hour; the smell of old flesh and decaying clothes made her sick. Then they came back renewed, with their trove of shells or bird's eggs, with eyes brightened from the sudden glimpse of a flock of rosellas.

Cathleen slept like a log. Sometimes Rosamund crawled into her bed and they toppled together into sleep. Her only fear was that it would come to an end. Mrs. Llewellyn was noticeably feebler each year. When Rosamund was three, she had a stroke, and overnight she was only half a person.

"She's like the half-chick in my book," said Rosamund to Florence, the friend she had found on the beach on one of their stolen outings.

So she was; it made Cathleen's lot more difficult, because the old lady was heavy as well as infirm. She had to be moved in and out of bed, washed like a child, supported. She can't last much longer, Cathleen thought.

But old Mrs. Llewellyn took a long time to release her grip on life. She had been ailing since her first stroke, which had left her paralysed down one side. Still she was brave and uncomplaining, and the side of her face that could still register emotion was always ready to smile. A horrible grimace, really, with one half of her face frozen as if by black magic, with froth at one corner of her lips, one eye fixed and unseeing. And the other side of her face, like a Cubist picture, merry as a pantaloon's, laughing at her own plight, rueful, but grateful for the gift of life.

Is it possible to want to live like that, Cathleen wondered. So hobbled, so thick-voiced, so dependent. Yet she saw the old face upturned to the sun, ancient sunflower, she knew that it was true, that old Mrs. Llewellyn was glad to greet the freesias in another spring.

Communication at the ordinary level was difficult. The words came so distorted and inappropriate from the twisted mouth, and her good hand, the right one, beat the side of her cane chair with such frustration that Cathleen wanted to weep for pity. Often it turned into a guessing game.

"It won't worry you if Rosamund has Florence to play? Sure?" Half a nod, half a smile; everything in halves. "Shall we go for a walk around the garden?"

The old woman leaned heavily on Cathleen's shoulder, stopped at the wisteria where the buds were discernibly swelling. "Thpring coming," she said, with an effort.

"I know," said Cathleen. "Isn't it beautiful! Lean on me. The children will pick some freesias for you. There's a great swathe of them out under the tree with the kookaburra's nest."

While the old lady dozed and dribbled in her chair, Cathleen took fair Rosamund and dusky Florence to the sliver of park next door, where the freesias grew wild. The two children tugged at the flowers, pulling them up bodily, bulbs and all, until Cathleen intervened.

"Gently, girls, gently. See, bend the stems back quickly and snap them off. Like this. We'll take the bulbs back to plant in our own garden."

A plover, two plovers, very fierce, were making their nest. Two magpies, even fiercer, gurgled and swooped low.

"They're chasing us," wailed Florence, putting her hands over

25

her head. But Rosamund stood her ground.

"Just paddle your toes in the shallow water, while I go and see if Mrs. Llewellyn wants anything." Cathleen waited while they seated themselves obediently on the fallen log, and busied themselves watching the tiny fish flicker under the wrecked boat in the mangrove swamp. "Don't move from the log. Promise?"

"Mamma," said Rosamund suddenly. "Why don't you send Mrs. Llewellyn away? She's a witch."

"She isn't. She's just sick. I told you before, it's her house, not ours, and I couldn't send her away if I wanted to. But I don't. She's very good and kind."

Lithe and supple, Cathleen ran barefoot under the grey gums, and climbed over the wire netting that hedged the garden. It was time to bring the old lady a cup of tea and a morsel of seed-cake to mumble around her gums.

But—her services were not required. Mrs. Llewellyn sprawled dead in her chair, her two eyes staring up blindly at the silver-gilt ball in the cobalt sky.

Death that had come so quickly and kindly on that exquisite spring day turned Cathleen's world upside-down. She scarcely dared to hope that the house had been willed to her—and yet, who else deserved it? Who else had washed the mountains of really disgusting linen—and sponged the old body clean (for the very old and very young are utterly incontinent). Who else had made scones and seed cake and swept up the crumbs that littered the floor after every meal? It seemed to Cathleen grotesque that five years of her own youth, that would never come again, had been spent in ministering to one so old.

I am sick of dying, I never want to go to another funeral in my life, she thought, mutinously. But because there was no one else to do it she made the funeral arrangements, and wrote to the great-niece, the fat kind young nurse who was now Mrs. Sampson, the mother of three children. She wrote to the sister in England (three girls at the turn of the century, there had been, only one left now). In Warwickshire she lived, the survivor, not far from Stratford, Cathleen noted. Not that it mattered.

Nobody answered the letters. So she used the money in the

tea-chest for the burial, and stripped all the flowers from the garden to make nosegays for the coffin. The funeral was less harrowing than she had imagined it would be, rather like a gathering of old friends and neighbours. Rosamund she sent to spend the day with Florence.

Twenty old-timers—more or less—came out of their tumbledown houses to pay their respects. Old Mr. Murgatroyd from the boat-shed (obsolete), Mrs. Potter who still owned half the land around Faggotter's Beach, the German couple from The Bower, the poet's spindly son—others Cathleen did not know. These were the friends who from time to time had called in on Mrs. Llewellyn, and they came now to pay their last call.

Oddly, Cathleen felt rather happy down at the cemetery; rueful, but glad that she was alive to feel the light spring breeze that ruffled the cabbage palms behind the tiny plot of ground, marked into little oblongs like a child's garden, most of the graves covered with flowers. It was peaceful and sunny among the crosses and plaster angels and November lilies flowering early. Mrs. Llewellyn's neighbours filed up to her for want of a better, and proffered condolences, which she accepted with lowered eyes, masking a sudden wild desire to laugh.

The minister, very pontifical, gave her a lift in his car, picked up Rosamund and deposited the two of them in their own garden.

When Rosamund was in bed, Cathleen set herself to the task of finding the will. For she was certain that somewhere, if she looked hard enough, there would be a scrawled document leaving her the house. A kind old lady after all, and a fair one; and very often she had said that Cathleen wouldn't regret her kindness. Fair is fair. The old sister in England—her roots were firmly set—and the great nieces, after all, had never come near. But although she searched, at first with guilt and then with rising fear as she tidied and sorted out Mrs. Llewellyn's possessions, there was no will. In the cedar writing desk, at last, next to a torn wedding photograph of a big-eyed, frightened girl—Mrs. Llewellyn?—and a young man with a moustache, she found a bundle of letters. The bottom one was the will. Quite briefly it stated the old lady's wishes: everything was to go to the two nieces. Blood was thicker, in the end, than water.

So that was that.

The two nieces came down from Brisbane to inspect their inheritance; from their disappointed faces it appeared that they didn't think much of it. Sisters, they were; one fat, one thin. The younger of the two, the kind young nurse of the maternity ward, was amiable and shabby, slack around the belly, but well disposed. Her sister was a well-dressed tartar.

"What will you do?" they asked.

"Stay on for a while," said the nurse, the one-time nurse. "Free."

The other one pulled her lips thin. "For a while, anyway. Till probate's granted. You can look around a bit. At least we won't have any bother with vandals if you're looking after things."

"What will you do with the house?" asked Cathleen, her eyes on the bay. "Sell it?" She had not realized until that moment how deeply she loved the old house, how urgent was her need for permanence, for belonging somewhere. "I wish I could buy it."

"Couldn't you?" asked the nurse. "It's pretty motheaten. We wouldn't want much."

"It's a valuable block of land, don't forget," said her skinny sister.

"Anyway, I haven't got any money," said Cathleen. "Just the little bit I get from giving piano lessons."

"What about your widow's pension?" asked the thin-faced woman.

Cathleen bit her lip. "Oh that!" she said. After a moment she added, "Rosamund goes to school this year. I might be able to get some sort of job in school hours—"

She would have no choice, it was a matter of necessity to get some steady sort of work when Rosamund went to school. Maybe as a housekeeper, she thought, for some widower, or a career woman who didn't want to wash the dirty dishes. Or in the beer garden, because they gave big tips there. Or in a convalescent home. But housekeeper would be better, because it meant somewhere to stay. Her lips drooped at the prospect of leaving this dear little house, with the garden she had made so charming, and the white carved verandah posts, and the beehive chimney.

28

The two sisters left, murmuring platitudes about being in her debt forever for her kindness to Auntie Marj, and assured her that if she could raise even a token deposit, that they would be glad to let her pay the house off year by year. Rather sourly, Cathleen thought that they were probably scared of white ants, and had decided that she'd be the only boob ready to take it on. She thanked them, and promised that she would think over their advice, which was to find someone in dire need of a housekeeper, and extort high wages, all the better to pay off this little house, which they would sell to her, in their magnanimity, for land value only. Self-interest can do strange things to people, Cathleen reflected. It was alright for me to work for nothing before, and now, when they want me to have money, they exhort me to fleece some human being in distress.

Still—it was spring! She would have a long vacation from being dutiful and unselfish.

I'm sick of being good, she thought, I'm sick of having no pretty clothes, and never having any money for anything. She had saved the money—such a pittance—that she earned from her handful of piano pupils. Piano was no longer in fashion; guitar was beginning to replace it. With a cheap guitar and a manual she might be able to teach herself well enough to take on a few children, just as long as she could keep one step ahead. But this summer, just this summer, she would go to the beach every day, soak up the sun, and teach Rosamund to swim, as her father had taught her when she was five, before he went away to war.

The children who came to make such awful noises on Mrs. Llewellyn's old upright piano came now with sarsaparilla dripping purple from their hands. It drooped as she put it in water; spilling opulently over dead stumps in the bushland, it did not take kindly to being yanked away.

Already, by October, it was possible to swim; so Cathleen took Rosamund and Florence to the beach, almost every day; a routine varied only on the days when the trade winds were so strong that they walked the mile around to the still water at the basin. Sometimes they were joined by Gert Levy, Florence's mother, healthy and cheerful and frankly forty-five, so busy and involved with a dozen small community services, so well-disposed towards the world, that it was pleasant to be with her.

She had a daughter of Cathleen's age, overseas; and eighteen years later, fate had allocated another one to her; Florence. She liked both her lives; she was as pleased to be working at Meals-on-Wheels with the old girls, she said, as to be picnicking with the young mothers. Cathleen had grown fond of her.

"You're so pretty, Cathleen," Gert said, again and again. "You'll have to marry again. Come to dinner and I'll rustle up someone nice for you."

But Cathleen always shook her head. She felt that she could never trust a man again; once bitten, twice shy, she thought, and she had been not only bitten, but chewed up and spat out.

One day Gertie brought her husband, jolly and lecherous, to share their picnic under the jacarandas at the basin. While the two children sorted their shells (how quickly their iridescence faded, out of the water) he kept trying to pinch Cathleen's behind.

Rosamund set one of the great yellow solandra cups on her tangle of yellow hair. "See, I'm a clown," she said, then took it off to look more closely. She traced the fine lines of purply-brown across the petals with delicate fingers, and passed it across to Cathleen. "It smells like apricots," she said. And so it did, like ripe apricots.

Gertie was back on the job. "You're too young to tie yourself to a memory.—Please, Tony, do leave Cathleen's bottom alone, you'll have her all the colours of the rainbow."

It was beautiful by the bay, with the jacarandas just coming into bloom, and sailor-boy daisies fighting it out with morning glories all the way down the cliff-sides.

Even more beautiful lay the sea—for the village was cradled between ocean and bay, bounded by hills, sun-warmed, embowered. Cathleen taught the two girls to swim in the rock pool, kept clean by the waves which washed over it twice a day. Old Jumbo lay under the peeling "Dogs Prohibited" notice, which everyone ignored; and sometimes groaningly got to his feet to investigate a morsel of dead fish or rotten sea-weed.

The sun shone benign and brazen from a cloudless sky, day after perfect day. It was the first summer since Cathleen had come to Alcheringa that she had hours to laze through. Time's spendthrift, she let the hours run through her fingers as carelessly as she did the sun-warmed sand. And she felt ripe as she had not felt ripe for five years. And after the summer—what? Let it wait, she thought, time enough later to come to terms with poverty.

Enriched now with the swelling rhythms of blossom and water, she found each day too short. She rose at dawn, when the birds tuned up. She worked in the garden until Rosamund woke to feed her pet hens—Chinese bantams, a gift from Florence. And then to the beach.

By the time the trade wind came up, at ten, they were ensconced on the beach, near the semi-circle of Norfolk Island pines. Rosamund grew golden-brown, the colour of good toast, and her beaky little nose was thick-dusted with freckles. Even when the holiday crowds came—ruining our village, everyone said crossly—they did not break their pattern. People Cathleen had passed in the shops, smiled at her now, because she was ready to smile at them. She felt the tenuous happiness of belonging, of committal, all the sweeter because perhaps it would be taken away from her.

Nobody wanted to take piano lessons in the holidays, so she was forced to dip into her savings.

But—how lovely it was, this life of the senses. She lay on the sand till she was scorching, then ran to dive in the waves, green as lemons, foaming, icy, making her nipples tingle, matting her hair.

When the shadows grew longer, as the cliffs hid the sun, they packed up; if it could be called packing; two towels, an empty bottle, a straw bag and an old dog.

And in their little house by the westerly bay the sun was still shining, and the splintery boards on the verandah warm under their feet.

They washed off the sand under the hose, she and Rosamund, and gathered the fruits of their garden; little mignonette lettuce, tomatoes, strawberries, bush lemons. A ripe paw-paw, from seeds they had dropped in the compost heap. Bananas, woody but sweet. Passionfruit. Three eggs from the six Chinese ladies, as Rosamund called them.

It was the cheapest way of living and the richest. Milk and meat and bread, a few groceries. Books from the free library. Rosamund discovered the magic poems of Eleanor Farjeon, and read them and re-read them until she could say them by

31

heart. Sometimes Cathleen played to her—how out of practice she was—syrupy pieces, like Nutcracker—And for herself she played the Debussy preludes that she loved. Sunken Cathedral—with its bells sounding from the land of dream. But when she tried to play The Afternoon of a Faun, she thought of Brian with his pointed ears and she pulled her fingers back from the keys as if they were scalding. That night she tossed and turned; so she kept away from the piano. Too disturbing, reminding her that Eden without Adam was a contradiction in terms.

Christmas came and went. Santa Claus (the newsagent dressed up) gave out ice-cream and balloons at the party on the beach that the shopkeepers turned on each year for their customers. The giant rockets and fiery cascades were fired from the sands as dusk came down; and the town children went in for a paddle and came out howling from blue-bottle stings. Living poor was living rich in the easy world of summertime.

With the thickening of the summer people, Cathleen moved down to the southern end of the beach, away from the beach flags and the transistors. The surf was more treacherous, swirling in odd cross-currents, but it was only a step away from the rock-pool. Another blessing, they were away from the ice-creams and fizzy drinks that every child seemed to be holding in his paws. Rosamund was rationed to one a day, and she accepted the rule more cheerfully if she did not see the day-long guzzlers. Cathleen came when she pleased, went home as she pleased. As the other mothers gathered up their fancy beach umbrellas and sunglasses—they said in voices of envy mixed with commiseration, "Lucky you, no man to cook for."

She had no beach finery; a plain, thin black costume, and a turquoise straw hat from Woolworths, that cast dappled shadows over her smooth forehead and flushed cheeks. She was brown and taut and slim, from working in the garden, and she was conscious of the admiration that attended her progress along the beach. She had plaited her brown hair, streaked with gold from the sun, into a pigtail, and tied it with a cherry-red ribbon.

This day, as all other days, she went for her last swim. She felt lithe and—yes, desirable—as she ran to towel herself dry. The beach had emptied. Cathleen glanced over her shoulder at the man who leaned on his elbow, patently admiring her; a man in middle age, portly but quite handsome. His two children were playing at the water's edge, squealing and running back as the waves came in; the little girl more venturesome than her bigger brother. The layers of peeling skin and suntan proclaimed them summer people. The woman had gone, picking up a beach-towel as big as a tent, and a cartwheel hat, a beautiful hat hung with wax peaches and grapes, tied with purple ribbons. Cathleen felt a stab of envy tinged with anger; such a plain hawk-faced woman, almost ugly, and the man so handsome. One of the things you see quite often, and always wonder about.

"I'll take the Jag, then," she said, swinging the car-keys. How insolently she walked, like someone who always knew where her next Jaguar was coming from. Slender long legs—from the back she was seductive.

But I am much prettier from the front, Cathleen thought, with satisfaction, and probably just about as good from the back too. It was years since she had thought about her looks, except for running a comb through her wavy hair, and reddening her lips, as a gesture. Now she turned boldly to meet his open admiration at close quarters.

"Is that your little sister?" he asked.

Cathleen felt herself flushing. Her cheap wedding ring was at home. She had bought it for herself quickly, without checking the size, and it was too big. She never wore it when she swam.

"It's my daughter," she told him.

"Well then, you were a child bride," he answered, ponderous but gallant, a little shy. "You can't be more than sixteen."

A coquetry she had not used for years bade her dissemble. She undid her plait, let her hair swing over her face, picked up a handful of sand and let it trickle through her fingers. She felt lazy and sensual, full of summer's sweetness, powerful.

"We're going back to town tomorrow," he told her. "But I can't imagine why I haven't noticed you before. You're very tanned—obviously you live around these parts."

The voices of the children, running in and out of the waves with their buckets, were faint.

"Soon I might have to live somewhere else," she said mournfully. "The old lady I was looking after just died, and I've got to find a new place, probably."

33

"Your husband?"

"I have no husband," said Cathleen, meeting his eyes levelly. For the first time in ages she allowed herself the luxury of self-pity. So unfair that some women—

One scream shattered the air; and another! Incoherent with fear the boy came running, came panting up. Rosamund? But Rosamund was safe. At the water's edge screaming, but safe. And the little head bobbing farther and farther each moment was someone else's child.

In one ungainly motion the man was on his feet, making for the water. She caught him, ran at his side.

"I can't swim," he panted, hopelessly. "But I'll have to try. Get the lifesavers—"

Get them? From four hundred yards away, where they watched by their reels, between the flags?

"You go!" said Cathleen, hitting him. "Quick! I can swim— But she's caught in the rip. Go back!" she screamed, as he hesitated. "I can't save both of you. Go back, Rosamund!" she screamed again and dragged the child whimpering, farther up the beach. "Stay there till I come back!"

She lunged into the water, dived under a wave, and was lost. The current dragged her whichways. All ways at once. She took a mouthful, surfaced. As the wave sucked her out, mercifully she banged against the child, flung out one arm, gathered it to her. Swim across the current, she recalled, let it take you out, then swim across. The child was a dead weight, senseless, that she held by her costume strap. With one arm she desperately kept them afloat, powerless against the forces that sucked at her life. Hang on, she told herself, soon—But soon would be too late—

The wave that picked them up and crashed them at the beach came just in time. Giant, it plucked them from the grasp of the lesser giant, tumbled them over and over, hurled them choking and half-dead on the sand.

For a moment Cathleen lay stranded, then she dragged the child higher up past the tide mark, turned it over, scooped sand from the dead mouth. Hopelessly she set herself to the task of bringing life back. For years, it seemed, she worked, ignoring Rosamund's cries, watching the water trickle, then spurt, feeling—thank God—life move beneath her hands. One, two—

release—wait. Yes, it was working, it was not too late. The shadows that fell across the two of them, rescued and rescuer, were the life-savers, and the frantic father.

"Here, I'll take over," said the boy with ginger hair. But the child was trying to sit up.

Only then was Cathleen able to indulge herself. She turned her back on them, trying to preserve the decencies still, and silently vomited into the hole next to Rosamund's bucket. She was shaking from terror at the thought of the might-have-been—how crazy can you be, to leave your own child unprotected while you dash in to play Grace Darling. I must have been mad, she thought, weakly, and started to cry.

The man was towelling his child dry, all the swagger gone from him. "I can never thank you enough," he said, very low. "If you hadn't been there, we'd have both been dead. How can I pay you back?"

"Never go away from the flags again," said Cathleen, with the ghost of a smile.

"Please. Isn't there anything I can do?"

Suddenly she dared. He was rich, she was sure; powerful, she was positive. She had risked her life to save his daughter, forsaken her own child who clutched at her now as if she would never let go. Flirtation was for children. This was for real.

"Find me a job. Somewhere I can keep my little girl."

"What can you do?" he asked, after a moment.

"Not much really. I can keep a house clean, and cook. I can teach children to play the piano, if I can find anyone who wants to learn. I was going to be a schoolteacher before I had my baby—"

He was smiling. "Dies mirabilis," he said. "Were you trained?—"

"Yes. But I never taught. I—"

"Did you finish your training?"

"Yes, but I told you, I never went out teaching. I was never even married," she whispered.

"No matter," he said, so powerful, so kind. "There's a job waiting for you. A girl as brave as you, and as steadfast—Don't tell me your secrets, I don't want to know. I'm one of the people at the top of that particular tree, as it happens. And I've never pulled strings before—to mix a metaphor—but this time I will."

4

He was as good as his word, the potentate, (for so he proved to be) ruler of the tight and circumscribed world which he inhabited. Nobody there was allowed to break rules, except the man at the top.

In no time, within the week, a letter came to summon Cathleen for a medical check-up; and she passed each test with ease. She was told to stand by: the department would place her as close to home as possible, on the lowest salary, and with the lowest status. But—what matter? She had found herself a job— a career, if she chose to work hard. With singing heart she wrote to the sisters in Brisbane: if they would take two of the three hundred pounds she had saved, as deposit, she would pay the house off, at first slowly, then, as her salary increased, as quickly as possible. She would live on the smell of an oil-rag, she vowed to herself, smiling to remember the words that her father had used to describe a miserly acquaintance. She held her breath as she waited for the letter that would tell her yes or no. It came. Yes, it said.

Cathleen hugged Rosamund to her until the child squeaked like a rubber doll, and laughed aloud to see her mother's joy. Everybody shared Cathleen's happiness, it seemed; she had not known she had so many well-wishers. The village solicitor, old Mr. Sharpe, pinched her cheek hard and promised to do her legal work for nothing, for the pleasure of seeing her bright eyes, he said. She sang for happiness as she worked around the house and garden—her own house now, nobody could turn her out.

At Gert Levy's there was much ado about the daughter's return from abroad. Gert planned a homecoming party, with bells on, she said, for the wandering girl she had not set eyes on for three years.

"Hope I can still recognise her," said Gert cheerfully. "Sometimes she's fat and sometimes she's skinny, and sometimes she's a blonde, then overnight she's got hair the colour of carrots." She laughed, full-bodied and contented in her laughter as in all things. "Now, no more arguments, Cathy, you're coming and that's that. Come naked, if you like, on second thoughts, that's a good idea. Just see you come, that's all."

Cathleen smiled and acquiesced. Gerty was not to be denied, adamant that Rosamund would bed down with Florence, while Cathleen played fast and loose with a dozen gorgeous eligible men, one of whom would sweep her off her feet and take her gondola-riding in Venice.

The queer thing was, it almost did happen that way. She felt diffident about her dress, a white sheath she had sliced out of cotton sharkskin and machined on Mrs. Llewellyn's old treadle monster. She was sure that it would single her out from the crowd of well-dressed, well-heeled women who made up Levy's clique. In the end it was only Rosamund's gusty pleadings that forced her to close the door on her little house, so shabby and peaceful, and venture out into a world much more garish, with values so different from her own.

She was amazed to find herself swamped with admirers. Her tan of rose and gold, her sun-streaked shiny hair held back with a blue band, brought forth a deluge of compliments. Flattery perhaps—words, idle words—but how charming to ears too long unused to badinage. She blushed, and was at once commended for blushing; deliciously, she could do no wrong. Even Rhonda, the belle (for after all she was Gerty's daughter, and the party in her honour) even Rhonda, swarthy and resplendent in a dress the colour of a peacock's tail, with an ostrich boa slung around her magnificent shoulders, even Rhonda, throwing back her chestnut head and displaying her really splendid teeth to all comers—even Rhonda Levy garnered no more courtiers. She sized Cathleen up with an expert's eye, the eye of one used to appraising, and said, "We'll halve the blokes, eh?"

That was how it worked out. A knot of middle-aged men, three shy and unattached young ones, plus a brash and charming Levy cousin formed Cathleen's court, handed her drinks, laughed at her jokes, begged her to dance, cut in—

How heady it was! The cold champagne bubbled, the four-piece combo made their jungle noises, the caviare and asparagus were offered and demolished. Under the spotlights, its improbable turquoise running a-banker with frangipani flowers, the new pool waited to be christened. How charming it

37

looked; and how absurd, with the bay only a stone's throw away, to have a swimming-pool as big as a ballroom in the backyard. Vulgar really, as well as redundant, but of course the Levys were so rich that they didn't know how to use up their money.

"Talk about bringing coals to Newcastle," cried Cathleen, very faintly tipsy. "With the bay so close you can pee—I mean peep—over the parapet."

A genuine slip of the tongue, but it made them all laugh, and repeat her sally. She tossed off her drink, and dared to tell them a rhyme, risqué and funny, set in the desert, where the Sphinx reigned as solitary queen. A burst of music from the bass guitar drowned the punch line, but they all roared with laughter. Begged to repeat it, she grew suddenly shy and shook her head.

By now it was a very noisy party. Short as a monkey and nearly as hairy, Tony Levy was doing a tango with a very tall divorcée. He was pumping her arm, pretending to be Groucho Marx; he didn't have to try very hard. His audience yelled for more. He obliged.

Gerty's minions, hired for the night, served the fabulous food that Gerty herself had prepared. Everybody stopped swilling and flirting, ready now for the more serious business of tucking in. Gerty sank back into a cane chair and surveyed her smash-hit party with satisfied eyes. She scooped up the compliments with aplomb, and repaid them with the wide warm smile that absolved her from the crime of being far too rich.

"Like it? I *am* glad," she said again and again as her guests commended the oyster patties, the round tables bedizened with hibiscus and tangerine candles, the improvised but near-perfect dance floor, the pool. "Oh, the trouble we had with this pool!" she cried, in her voice as loud as a tocsin. "The bulldozer man came back one night with a bunch of his mates. It was the night of the black-out. He wanted them to have a look-see at the biggest 'ole they ever seen. He was so drunk!"

"Say no more, Gerty," someone begged. "Is he pushing up daisies?"

"No way!" said Gerty Levy. "God tempers the wind to the shorn lamb, as they say. The lights went out before I could get outside to order him off. I heard a crash and a yell, then his friends were leaping down after him. The cement was in, but not the water, you see—" She waited for the laughter to stop. "They were all begging him to speak to them, Bert ole son—"

"And did he?"

Gert took a swig of her drink, and began to chuckle. "From both ends! His swearing was only matched by his farting, as his pals dragged him along the bottom of the pool. He smelled like a sewer-truck and howled like a banshee. But for all that he only ended up with a broken leg."

Everyone was hysterical, everyone was drunk. Hard-eyed business men, plump matrons, girls and boys, all of them. A woman in a red caftan jumped in the pool, drowning the frangipani, and one by one they followed like silly sheep. Submerged, or half submerged, they began to shed their clothes.

Cathleen watched with the clarity of a visitant from another planet: one is isolated by being the only sober person at a drunken rort. She didn't want to join in; really most of them would have done better to keep their clothes on. She dodged a Givenchy pyjama suit, rolled into a sodden ball and flung at random. Rhonda was nowhere to be seen. The group of young couples seemed to have slipped away into the dark recesses of the garden, no doubt to do just that, to couple, thought Cathleen wryly. The pool was filled with middle-aged bodies, and a very nasty sight it was.

I don't want to be part of this, thought Cathleen, I wish I hadn't come. Quickly, surreptitiously, she edged behind the marquee, then over the flagged terrace to the French doors that led through a library, never used, to a music room just as superfluous. Her fingers caressed the only possession of the Levys which she coveted, their beautiful grand piano. Nobody played it now—had anybody ever played it? It was in tune, anyway.

The sounds of the party, intermittently rising and falling, reached her from a distance, discernible but remote. She ran her fingers over the keys, of course it would be in tune, Gerty would see to that. Very quietly she began to play, letting her fingers guide her brain, until they strayed into a fragment of Debussy, the Sunken Cathedral. She played on, remembering forgotten sea-sounds, recalling with sudden sharpness the green of sea-grapes, quivering under water, remembering long-ago bells,

39

heard over water, remembering the sea.

As her hands came to rest someone stood breathing behind her, someone bent over and put his lips against the nape of her neck.

"Alice in Wonderland," he said, the rich Levy cousin. "That was beautiful. You're beautiful. Play me some more." When she shook her head he didn't persist. "I didn't know that girls still washed their faces and played the piano. Not these days. Gee, I wish I'd met you before, Cathy. I'm going to Europe next month."

Her heart, stupidly, fell. "Oh, are you? Lucky you! For how long?"

"A year or so. On business for my firm. All over Europe. How about coming with me?" His eyes, hooded and Semitic, met hers in open avowal.

Party talk, persiflage. Yet he seemed to mean it. She matched his gaze for a long moment, then lowered her lids. "No thank you," she said primly. "Next month I start work. I'm going back to school."

"School?" He was abashed, then recovered. "Yeah, I thought you were a schoolgirl. But tell me, have you reached the age of consent?"

She tried, but could not help laughing. "I'm a teacher. I am. Truly!" When he shook his head and refused to believe she grew indignant. "I'm a widow!" she cried. Or a grass widow, or a de facto, or at least some one *experienced* she wanted to add. Of course she said none of it. Instead she stood up. "I've suddenly discovered that I've got a headache, and I want to go home. I want my own bed."

"You and me both," said the cocky young man. "No, sorry, I didn't mean to offend you. I take it back. Consider it unsaid."

Cathleen pushed past him, and went to say her goodbyes. The pool still swarmed with half-naked bodies. Proud, it seemed, of their sagging breasts, women stood waist-deep in water; men, somewhat taller, took the water-line across their slack bellies. Cathleen averted her eyes from the spectacle they were making of themselves. Unseemly old idiots, she thought, uncharitably. On the side of the pool sat a naked woman of perhaps sixty, with grizzled pubic hair and whitish mottled thighs. She was telling a salacious anecdote of a weekend visit to a nudist camp.

40

"I was so proud of Ernest!" she shouted. "He was the only man there with an erection!"

Screams of laughter, inhuman laughter, rewarded her, screeches like sea-gulls fighting over food, rosellas squabbling. But sea-gulls are exquisite in flight, thought Cathleen, and rosellas a kaleidoscope. Not like these sad remnants—oh how can they bear the sight of each other? She turned away. Wine bottles had been knocked over, and trickled red on to the white tablecloths. Cigarettes were stubbed out on the hibiscus blooms. Spilled food, squashed bits of lobster and blobs of creme brûlée were slopped across the lawns.

"Thank you, Gerty, it was great fun," whispered Cathleen. "But I have to go now. I'll get Rosamund tomorrow."

"Night-night, angel," said Gerty, still dressed, but dripping wet. "Is Basil driving you?"

"No," said Cathleen. "I'm walking."

"I'm walking too," said Basil, falling into step beside her.

"It's over a mile. You'll be sorry."

"It's a beautiful night," he replied. After a while he added, "I think I'll be glad."

A beautiful night it was, very clear, the sky a dark blue funnel, or tunnel, the stars thick-clustered. Under their feet bark scrunched, leaves crumbled and gave back a sharp tang of lemon.

"That smell of lemon—there must be a lemon gum near here. It's still shedding its bark." She looked up and saw it, most graceful of trees, waving thin leaves above them. "It's called Eucalyptus citriodora," she told him, pedantic in her desire to head him off from the declaration he seemed about to make.

He gave a grin, very sure of himself, prepared to wait. "How really fascinating!" he mocked her. The strong lines of his face were defined and enhanced by starlight. "Are you going to give me a botany lesson, little schoolteacher?" He took her hand in his and swung it as they walked. "Seriously, why haven't I met you before? Gerty's always trotting out new girls, trying to make an honest man of me. How did she come to miss you?"

"Because I've been too busy working until now to have time for jollity. Anyway Gerty's world isn't mine. It's just that our children are friends."

"You're lying again," said Basil Levy. "First you pretend that

41

you're a schoolmarm, now it's a mother. What next? Grandmother? Vampire? Member of Parliament? Come on, I'm easy, I'll believe anything you tell me."

In the night air so sweet and balmy, heavy with oleanders, their laughter chimed. She did not answer.

"Seriously, Cinderella," he said, grave, or assuming gravity. "Where have you been hiding? And what sort of a job is it that keeps you from—what did you call it?—jollity?" With the ease that comes from long practice he lifted her hand to his lips, and kissed her fingers lightly before he released them. "Wait—wait a minute—it's all falling into place. You're the gorgeous child with a gorgeous child Gerty was talking about. And by God, she's right! You *are* gorgeous!"

"Thank you," said Cathleen sedately, turning the last corner before her own house came in sight. She shook her head to his offer of a cigarette.

"No? So you don't smoke, practically don't drink—you don't—er—"

"Fornicate?" Cathleen murmured the rather archaic word in a silky voice. "No. Once, maybe. But that was in another country—and—"

He cut her short. "You know what, Cathy? I'd really like to take you with me. No malarky. You've never been? I reckon I could get you smuggled over on the expense account."

Surely he was joking? Some joke, thought Cathleen, sourly. "Please don't make fun of me."

"Who says I'm making fun? Listen, I've been looking all my life for a girl who doesn't put muck all over her face.—Venice," he tempted her. "Paris. The Black Forest.—Come on, what have you got to lose?"

"It's just that—Well, this contract is too unadvised, too sudden," she quoted.

He took her literally. "What contract?" he asked in alarm, quite nonplussed. "Don't get me wrong."

"I was quoting," said Cathleen. "I didn't misunderstand your offer, I assure you."

At ease again, he was ready to importune her. "Who knows how it'll all turn out? We might even end up—well, there's no saying where we might end up," he said cagily. "Come on, Cathy. If you don't like the deal you can have your ticket and take off home. How's that?"

They had crossed the park, all tall trunks and pools of shadow, and halted at her gate. Cathleen looked up, measuring him. "I suppose you take a new playmate every trip?"

He did not deny it. "Why not? Only—"

"Only what?"

"Who knows? This time it mightn't come unstuck."

She wrenched open the gate. "I can't be bought!" she cried, quite violently, because in one way she wanted to stay. With the part of her that was still the girl who had so ardently responded to Brian's ardours she wanted to say yes, quickly, before he changed his mind. She was tired of being prudent and unselfish and living for next week and next year, sick and tired of having all her eggs in one basket. Addled eggs maybe, who could tell? When she gazed at the prospect he placed so alluringly before her, she was almost ready to up and follow.

"I can't possibly come. I've got a job to do, and a child to look after. And a house to pay for." She held her breath. Perhaps he would say that Rosamund could tag along, too.

He said no such thing, of course. Instead he leaned so hard on the rickety gate she had shut on him that he broke a hinge. "See," he said. "Even your gate is asking me in. Can I come in?"

"No! Not for a second!" said Cathleen firmly, and pushed it shut.

He gave a deep sigh, then a snort of laughter. "I didn't even get in for the first," he said impudently. "But I'll try again."

And so he did. By telephone he wooed her, besought her with brash beguilements. How nearly she said yes. Except for Rosamund she would have capitulated. For what girl in her right senses would want to stay home and teach kids with runny noses when she could be fronting the Taj Mahal by moonlight?

"No," she said, again and again. "It's too absurd. You don't know anything about me. I might snore."

"By the way—do you?"

"Certainly not."

At no time did he mention Rosamund: clearly she was no part of the deal. Would Gerty keep her as a companion for Florence for, say, three months? Furiously she pushed the thought away. No way she would fob her child off, even for a snatch of time. Somehow she knew that Rosamund would never forgive or forget what would seem to her desertion.

"You could buy your clothes over there. In Paris."

It wasn't fair, he was using his riches to buy her. Across the room, held in a shaft of sunlight, dirty-faced, Rosamund was whining for attention. She had trodden on a thorn, and thought she might be poisoned.

Cathleen put her hand over the mouthpiece, hot from her breathing. "Oh, do be quiet," she said irritably. "I'll come and fix it in a minute. Get your paints." She took her hand away and spoke into the telephone. "No, there's nobody here. I was just talking to the cat." Feeling herself observed, she turned to see Rosamund's eyes, rounded in disbelief. Her gaze was a douche of cold water, sobering Cathleen, shocking her into reality.

She took a deep breath. "It wasn't the cat," she said, her voice wobbling a trifle. "It was my little daughter. And I'd better stop pretending to myself as well as to you. I can't possibly leave her. And I can't give up a good job for a whim. Even a whim as seductive as that one."

"Live dangerously," said the tempter's voice, the voice from the faraway vaults of pleasure she would never inhabit. "Put her into boarding-school. You'll get another job. One way or another, I'll find you a job—" So glib, so practised in his allurements, so sure that he would prevail.

"No!" She spoke more harshly than she intended, because she had come to look forward to his calls, depend on them, even. "It'd all break up. You'd leave me in the lurch, or something. And then I'd have another baby, or something. It's all absurd! I can't and I won't, so don't ring me again, please."

"If that's how you want it," he said coldly, and slammed the telephone down.

So, naturally, that was the end of that.

44

5

Life gives with one hand, takes with the other. This is one of the lessons of growing up. Nothing is, or can remain perfect. Every good has its companion bad, inevitable shadow, thought Cathleen, as she settled into her new life as an ex-student teacher of somewhat ripe years. It was wonderful to have a regular cheque paid every second Thursday, as surely as the sun rises. Not very big, but very sure. Yet the other side of the coin was that it had to be worked for steadily, even grindingly, day in, day out; and in those sybaritic weeks of pleasing herself she had grown out of the habit of pushing on against her will. And she was so inept: she made so many mistakes, such elementary ones, in compiling her roll, in making up her register, even in allowing the children to go to the lavatory at times that were taboo, just before playtime, or just after lunch.

"But what if they *need* to go?" she asked. And the answer from the powers above, delivered with calm certainty, was always the same, that they must learn to wait. Often, since they had not learned, they wet on the floor, and Cathleen, mopping up, looking at the drenched eyes and the drenched pants, felt all kinds of a brute.

She liked the children of Cabbage Tree, country children many of them, Italians and Yugoslavs from the outlying farms. Rosie, they called Rosamund. "Her name too long, missus," as one black-eyed urchin told her. So Rosie it was. As for the teachers, they were a mixed bunch. The headmistress was Scottish, red-haired, thin, brisk, impersonal, with bright grey eyes as hard as marbles; fenced off from beauty by her big buck teeth, she set no store on looks, affected to despise them. Did she know Cathleen's story? She gave no sign. Communication between them was limited to criticism of Cathleen's mistakes, a bevy of them, a spring that never ran dry. No experience in teaching rhythm? Or verse-speaking? She clacked her teeth together.

"What's verse-speaking?" asked Cathleen gauchely.

"Verse-speaking, Mrs. Bell, is the subject you have to teach *my* class on Tuesday and Thursday, when your kindergarten children have gone home."

45

Some help, thought Cathleen, with a gleam of humour. "Thank you," she said meekly. She would ask the deputy, so wheezy, but so kind. With such a terrible breath, but so kind.

"The other three days you will take rhythm for the other three classes. Miss Jones will take her own. Your piano playing is fairly good," said the voice of judgment.

"Thank you," said Cathleen. Cathleen McKinnon, A.Mus.A. "I'll do my best."

The deputy, Miss Jones, was very sympathetic, quick to offer her own collection of poems suitable for setting to rhythmic movements.

"That's all verse-speaking is. Don't be frightened. Have you any finger-plays, dear?"

"What are they?" Another thing to learn. Every minute another thing to learn.

"Don't look so appalled, pet," said this kind old maid. "I'll bring you mine to copy out." She was quite sentimental about children, even after years and years of teaching them. She found Rosamund a darling, she said. A changeling-child, she called her, with her odd blend of fantasy and feet-on-the ground. If she knew Cathleen's story she gave no sign. Cathleen was the only married woman on the staff—they all believed or elected to believe her fiction—and by far the youngest in that plain and manless seraglio.

It had all been arranged so quickly, so smoothly, with such aplomb and finesse. From the first long official envelope that summoned her to an interview, to the appointment at this small school in the neighbouring township, it was only a matter of weeks. The question of her bond (for technically she had defaulted, and the bondswoman, her mother, was dead) somehow that was arranged, too.

The day after Basil made his last bid, and she gave her last answer, she was summoned again to the building in Bridge Street where the appointments were handed out.

A forward young clerk, whose wedding-ring didn't cramp his style in the least, gave her the eye as he told her that everything had been arranged. "The boss says it's all fixed up for you to go to Cabbage Tree, if that suits you. Say, who are you? A princess

46

incognito, or something. My boss got his orders from v-airy high up. We've been told to get out the red carpet for you."

Cathleen shook her head. "I'm nobody. From nowhere."

From the photograph in a newspaper wrapped around the potatoes she had learned the name of the man who had pulled strings for her. Golly, she thought, looking at the dark distinctive face, no wonder he said he was at the top of the tree. She mooned over the face for a moment, toying with the might-have-been. Say the woman had been swept out too, and I couldn't get her in, just the little girl. And say he came back looking for me afterwards, all upside-down the way you are when somebody dies. Stupid, she thought, crumpling the paper. I've had enough of romantic tomfoolery that leads nowhere except to heartbreak. From now on, she vowed, everything I do will be sensible, and before I take any step into any unknown country, I will test the ground with my feet, for quicksands.

So here she was, what her mother (perhaps not her father) had wanted her to be, a little schoolmistress, safe in a niche, protected by the all-sheltering wings of the Government. Here she was ensconced (enslaved?)—unbelievably a person of property. I could go on a jury, she said to herself, with a snort of amusement.

"I will be good," she said solemnly to Rosamund, who had come to track down the sound. "That's what Queen Victoria said. I'm laughing because we're going to make it, you and I."

"Queen Victoria is in my book of Kings and Queens," said Rosamund. "But the one I like best is Piers Gaveston. He was King Edward's friend."

"Trust you!" said Cathleen, hugging her wilful pretty child, who liked the green rind of the watermelon better than the red stuff, as she called it; and unerringly lighted on the one homosexual in a fairly stuffy collection of English monarchs and their courts. "School tomorrow. Both of us. I wonder how we'll make out?"

How hard she worked, trying to fit herself to the role the headmistress assigned to her. How carefully she prepared her lessons, how humbly she accepted criticism, how modestly she dressed. With what bated breath she awaited the result of her first inspection. She was hardly installed before they sent an inspector out to look at her work, a man, thank goodness.

47

"Very good indeed!" he pronounced, twirling his moustache and smiling down at her as if he thought her a good-looking girl as well as a good teacher. "Um—your appointment is—um—irregular—but you are coping very well. Very well indeed."

She glowed back at him. "I thought you'd come to give me the sack."

He gave a creaky sort of laugh. "Oh no, we're not all monsters." His shrewd eyes said that he knew her secret. She felt suddenly uneasy; she was glad when the headmistress bustled in.

Oh, but how tired she was at the end of each day, gathering up a pile of work to be prepared, Easter rabbits to be traced for wall-friezes, Empire Day costumes to be prepared for a pageant, Safety First posters to be worked out, a hundred things. Each night she fell into bed, and slept the dreamless sleep that goes with untroubled mind and dog-tired body.

Rosamund—Rosie—was happy too. At first she had missed Florence, who went to Alcheringa school; but soon she had a retinue. As teacher's child she had a ready made place; and although at first she showed off in class and vied for her mother's sole attention, she soon gave it up as a bad job. The headmistress had impressed on Cathleen that at school her child must be treated as one of a class, no more. Rosamund pouted at first, but accepted the dictum when Cathleen told her that without the job there'd be nothing to eat.

"We could be like Hansel and Gretel and the gingerbread house," Rosamund suggested.

"No," said Cathleen firmly. "We couldn't. Just be a good girl, will you, darling? Call me Mrs. Bell at school. Please."

So at school Rosie called her Mrs. Bell; and at home Rosamund called her mummy. When she was good she was very very good, and, thank God, at the moment she was on the side of the angels. She was a dreamy child, clever and sharp as a pin when she wanted to be, but mostly woolgathering. Celestial fleece, thought Cathleen, looking at the finger-painting (starch and raw colour, four pots to a table) that was like no one else's. She scooped out gobbets and swirled them together to make patterns of purply-brown and raw orange that had nothing to do with the subject: my mother shopping. Her fingers whirled

48

furiously until the paper was sodden, and all the paint used up, and the others at the table complaining.

"What does it mean?" asked Cathleen, perplexed. "Where are the people shopping?"

"That's the hot sky, see. There's the sun, see. That's the cruel magpie that dive-bombs the people, see he's happy."

"Where are the people, Rosie?"

"He killed them. With his beak," said Rosamund, who would never be Rosie in a million years. When the children started to laugh she looked up in surprise and laughed with them.

Well then, thought Cathleen, deeply proud, deeply disturbed, she has inherited her father's talent. For talent he did possess, by all accounts. Once in a while Cathleen lighted on his name in a newspaper. Once it was a name listed among others in an account of a colony in Greece, a group of young expatriates. Once he had a column to himself, a long article on his first exhibition in London, which caused a minor furore, according to the correspondent. Whatever that meant. So he has made it after all, she thought, with a wintry clutch of breath: no old man, or old woman, of the sea to weigh him down. I don't care, she said to herself, disconsolate, envious. For in Greece it would be warm, hot even, and here it was cold, cold. Indian summer had come and gone, the hot June days that were the prelude to winter. The garden lay bowed beneath the drenching rains of July. Fallen leaves squelched sodden, wet hens huddled inside their pen, the bay stretched leaden under leaden skies.

It took a hefty effort of will to don mackintosh and gumboots, and slop across the park to the bus stop, to look out of the misted windows at the drowned world that the bus was bisecting, with thundering breakers on one side, grizzling bay on the other. She laboured up the hill to Cabbage Tree with Rosamund whimpering beside her, towards a classroom that smelled of wet children and wet clothes. As for her own house, it leaked in a dozen places. Next year she would have to afford repairs, somehow. Next year she would earn a little more, maybe fifty or a hundred pounds.

Sometimes, however, even in those unending weeks of rain, it was snug. On a Friday night, when the fire stopped smoking and the pine-cones glowed red, when they sat on the hearth-rug, the two of them, and ate oranges, while Jumbo snored his life away, the pattern of Cathleen's days seemed tranquil and comely.

"Mummy, why don't I have a father like Florence and all the other kids?" asked Rosamund one night.

"Children, not kids." Cathleen played for time. "He went away," she said, presently.

"To heaven?" asked Rosamund, who was very strong on heaven since she had been going to Sunday-school with Florence.

Was Greece heaven? He probably thought so. Painting yourself dry under a blue sky was probably a pretty good facsimile, anyway.

"Yes," said Cathleen, tampering with the truth. "I daresay you could call it heaven."

"Has he got wings?" Rosamund was preparing to explore the subject at depth, a stubborn matter-of-factness blended with her flight of fancy.

"I shouldn't think so," said Cathleen. "Oh look, the pine-cones are all used up, get me another armful, that's a good girl. Would you like some cocoa?"

"Can I go to stay with Florence next week? Her mother's nice. Florence spilled cocoa all over her mother's new silk parasol, and her mother just laughed. She said plenty more where that came from."

Cathleen changed her yes to no. Better to woo Rosamund from the land of everything-laid-on. "No. But she can come here if you like."

"She likes coming here," said Rosamund. "She says it's like a doll's house."

From Gert Levy came disturbing news: Basil was dead. Killed in a plane crash in Turkey, Gert said. Cathleen was desolate for a moment: Basil so young, so impudent, so full of life. Then she sucked in her breath at the narrowness of her own escape.

6

How the year flew. First it dragged, and then it flew. No sooner had they plummetted into winter, come to terms with it, then it was spring again, and Rosamund was six.

It was her first party. Six little girls in party dresses, six candles on a cake with pink icing; balloons and hide and seek behind the willows. Pin the tail on the donkey. Oranges and lemons. Squeals and sticky faces, and someone howling from toothache. The mothers came to deliver their children by car, even those living quite close, and again to pick them up, as if legs weren't meant for walking. Pressed, the children gabbled thankyouforhavingme, all in a breath, and waved goodbye. Rosamund was collecting her loot, and gloating over the two black dolls which she had instructed Florence to buy for her. The coloured pencils were nice, yes;—but she liked the dolls best of all. Her twins, she called them.

"Don't you like all those tubes of paint?" Cathleen was disappointed. They were good paints, very expensive.

"Yes, I do. But I wanted those dolls more than all the world," said Rosamund. Sensing her mother's puzzlement she glanced up. "I'll paint a hundred pictures for you tomorrow," she offered.

"Thank you," said Cathleen.

In a bound it was Christmas. Different, this one, from last: safer, but stodgier. Cathleen was wrung-out, skinny and bone-tired when the holidays started. She went to the beach obediently, with her daughter, but all the sparkle seemed to have gone out of her. Her costume, the same old black one that was going to last forever, hung loosely on her. Her hair was lifeless. No one whistled after her, and she was glad. There was no bounce left in her step: the inroads of the year had used her up.

Sometimes she stayed at home, puttying up holes, painting thirsty boards, cleaning windows. Little by little, as her skills increased, the house began to gleam. Jenny Jones down the road found an old pensioner for Cathleen, glad to make a few shillings, gladder still to have someone to listen to his hoard of stories.

51

He sat over his cup of tea, dunked biscuits in it, then poured it into the saucer and drank noisily. Yes, sure as eggs he remembered Alcheringa in the old days, most of the old hands gone now, all but a few. That there poet had a farm near Faggotter's beach, his missus was a bit of a tartar, strong though, she could work like a bullock when she put her mind to it. Yes, there used to be a dairy on the other side of the big hill, there's some flash guys come cutting it up into little blocks, but they'll never be able to use the other side, too steep. Old man Rutherford he owned all that land round the school, they're making that into house-land too, pity, he said, running his tongue around his false teeth. He droned on, so long-winded that Cathleen almost paid him off. Yet his stories had a flavour all their own, she thought, and went on listening.

"The war took a lot of the boys, the first war, that is," he said. "They nearly all went. Four of the Mason boys was killed."

"Four?" Cathleen was horrified.

"They still had eight left," he said. "Not that the old lady ever stopped grieving—"

Sometimes he seemed to her a poet, sitting there in his stinking grey flannel shirt, telling his stories of people long turned to dust. "Couldn't keep a thing to yourself in Alcheringa in the old days, everyone knew when Bob Black was sweet on the new teacher. Pretty as a picture, she was."

"Did they get married?"

He gave his rheumy laugh. "Course not! Fat chance! He was already tied up good and proper. His missus took a horse-whip to the girl one night, nearly scared the daylights out of her. She wouldn't give him the time of day, after—" His faded eyes looked past her into times long gone. "Lived in the old dairy on the rough side of the hill, for a while, Bob did, he was a horny bloke, begging your pardon. Dead now, these many years. Gone to rack and ruin the old place has, belongs to one of them blokes that chops up stone with a chisel. He doesn't come there much."

"A stone-mason?"

"Yeah. No. Something in that line." The flies buzzed around the window as he unwound his long skein of memory, knees planted apart, watery eyes blinking. "Tell you what you'd have liked, missus, the old days when they swum the young cattle, vealers they was called, swum 'em over to the Basin to the green grass. Bob Black, he used to take 'em up the dirt road, choose a calm day and off they'd go, their mothers mooing like all-get-out. It was a sight you'd never forget, all them horns sticking out of the water, my word they was bushed when they scrambled out. Wonder the sharks didn't get 'em."

Rosamund was tapping at the window, trying to attract her mother's attention. Behind her, Florence and Timmy were fighting over the swing, squashed side by side, each refusing to vacate it.

"I must go," said Cathleen, standing up. "I'm afraid I've kept you from your work," she added, to remind him of jobs left undone.

"That's alright. I like to have a good yarn." He put his dirty felt hat on his bald head and stumped out. While he ripped out the wooden planks with dry-rot he entertained himself with mournful hymns.

The children laughed at him behind his back. It was their pleasure to pretend that he was a bogey-man: it added spice to their day. They pelted each other with bush lemons, from a tree so burdened that its thorny branches touched the ground. They had an old canoe that they paddled around the mangrove clumps, where the tide came in full. They rowed from sun into dappled shade, around the sunken boat, each year more rotten. They said it was a pirate's ship, filled with sunken treasure.

Was she happy? Cathleen hardly knew. She was always busy, often tired. Sometimes she thought of her father with a great surge of longing: someone to approve of all she did, someone to look at her with eyes wholly loving, someone committed, with nothing held back. It is only parents who wear that face of love, thought Cathleen. I wore it for Brian, then our paths diverged. I wanted this path, he wanted that one. So in the end it was a mask of love I wore. But some day, who knows, some day—My mother loved my father forever. Who knows what life holds for me?

"Aren't you lonely by the bay?" the teachers asked her. "Aren't you frightened?" Lonely, yes, sometimes. Frightened, no. Sometimes she toyed with the idea of taking a lodger, but the house was so tiny, four little rooms and two slivers of verandah. It just wouldn't work.

Extravagantly, on impulse, she bought a secondhand record-player. Rosamund should grow up with music, not just her mother at the piano, but all manner of beautiful sounds. They lay in bed on hot summer nights and listened, Rosamund running from her own room to hear the translucent counter-tenor of Alfred Deller singing Elizabethan lyrics in a voice so pure that it was disembodied. Tears of happiness wet Cathleen's cheeks as she listened to Ariel's songs from The Tempest. But when he sang of lovers sundered, of anguish and languish, she turned her face into the pillow. He sang of love's languors and of love betrayed; and suddenly she could bear no more. She scrambled over Rosamund in her haste to silence the voice that laid bare old wounds. In the sudden silence after song she heard her own breathing, rough and shallow.

Their park was so quiet that it was almost an extension of the garden. Cathleen planted masses of the stumpy Persian iris under the grey gums, and cuttings of honeysuckle. Mrs. Llewellyn's big single white rose sprawled over the lichened fence and up the Sydney peppermints. The possums ran down the trees and across the park to steal her grapes; always, in winter, one possum came to sleep in her roof, then, later, another. Soon there was a family in part-time residence, hissing at Rosamund's attempts to pat them. In time they came to take bread from her finger-tips.

Florence and Rosamund, parted at school, were inseparable at holiday times. One autumn Gert Levy asked Cathleen to take care of Florence while she tripped off to Hawaii with Tony.

"I'd offer to pay you, Cathy, love, but I know you'd scream. But I'll bring you back something smashing—"

"Rosamund will be ecstatic," said Cathleen, stifling her own twinge of envy. "I'll be glad to have her. But I wonder that you're not frightened of flying after Basil's crash."

"Don't mention it!" Gerty was going, by hook or by crook. "Qantas is safe, they all are, really. And if I come down in flames, you'll just have to bring Florence up for me."

Some people get orchid leis, some get dirty handkerchiefs to wash out. Scarcely had her mother gone than Florence was sneezing. Rubbing the wheezy chest at night with camphor, Cathleen felt herself hard done by. Hosts and guests, she had read somewhere: life divides people into these two categories.

Like it or not, she was stuck with the role of host.

When Florence recovered, they went to films, to the beach, for walks. The girls were charmed by a tiny house with an arched gateway, all stuck-over with shells. Rosamund swore that an old fisherman lived there, a man with no shoes and a bag on his back with monkeys in it. She said that she had seen him at low tide one evening, with monkeys' faces poking out of the sack. The house was full of monkeys, she insisted.

"His father was a poet," Cathleen told them. "He was the one with a monkey on his back."

Down in the park, where the morning glory and lantana grew thick, there was a hollow made by the town drunk. Quite often they came on him lying there, an empty bottle by his side, his mouth a-dribble, his eyes closed, snoring.

"Poor man," sighed Cathleen, quelling the children with a glance. "Be sorry for him. He's had a hard life, I think. Try to be sorry for people like that."

Very virtuously they said that they would try: Florence added that she thought she might be a missionary when she grew up; Rosamund was sorry that she hadn't thought of that notion first.

One day they took their dolls to the park for an airing. Cathleen, busy with the ironing, did not notice how the time had passed. Four o'clock. Where were they? She tidied herself and went in search. Not there? No doubt they had gone up the hill to the big park, with its swings and see-saws. She took off after them, following the path they must have taken. No, not there. At the school, then? Although they had been told, over and over, that they must never play in the schoolground when school was out—

"Have you seen Rosamund?" she called to the children on the swings.

No one had seen. Suddenly Cathleen was sure that she knew the answer: they had gone to look at the shell-gate. She crossed the road and cut through the paddock where the horses were grazing, and down a side street. She was uneasy, rather than alarmed: sensible little girls, both of them. She ran under the archway, and up to the house with its chimney thick with shells. The door was open.

"Rosamund! Florence!" She went inside. Nobody was there,

55

no one at all.

She was really frightened now. It was two when they had gone. Now the shadows were long. She began to run. The man next door looked curiously at her.

"Were two little girls here? One fair and one dark?"

He shook his head. "I've been working in the garden since lunch-time. There's no one come here."

She started for home, trying to calm herself. No doubt they had met Sara or Liz, or somebody from school. Nothing to worry about. But soon it would be dark. Should she ring the police?

Steven from her class was walking home with his sister. "Have you seen Rosamund?"

"Yes," said his sister. "Rosie and Flo, they were taking the drunk man home."

Cathleen stood still. They were—or was he taking them? "Where does he live? Tell me! Quick!"

"Oh, somewhere in a shed near the tennis court," said Steven.

Cathleen turned back, and began to run. My fault, she accused herself: my fault for telling them to trust everyone. My fault for being jealous of Gerty. Whatever happens, my fault.

"Look!" called Steven. "There they are!"

Very grubby, very insouciant, Rosamund and Florence were coming out of the driveway from the tennis-courts. They were nursing their dolls and chattering.

"Oh, you terrible child!" Cathleen flew at Rosamund and shook her. "Where did you go?"

Rosamund was bewildered. "We just took that poor man home, because he couldn't walk straight."

"We were being missionaries," said Florence.

And the years slid away. Rosamund lost her baby teeth; the great big ones that pushed them out were too big for her little face. Cathleen found her first grey hair. At twenty six a grey hair? Horrified, she wrenched it out.

"Can I go to ballet lessons?" demanded Rosamund. "All the kids go."

"Girls. Girls, not kids."

"Girls. Can I?"

"Yes, you may." Cathleen capitulated, joined the line of

mothers warming the benches, waiting for the Saturday dancers in leotards and ballet shoes. Rosamund was rather heavy, but comely and controlled in her movements; she caught her mother's eyes and smiled back, happy among her peers.

Now she was eight. Absurd. It was only a minute since she had butted her way into the world. Infants' school was behind her, before she had even started, it seemed. And the day after she turned eight she was nine, and the day after that, ten.

She was sick of ballet, she said, she hated it. She wanted to change to physical education, fizzy as she called it. All the girls hated ballet, all the girls loved fizzy. So leotards were out.

At ten she was tall and fair, still besotted with fairy-tales. When she went to the children's library she came back with books enough to furnish her with a week's supply of dreams and nightmares. Gaunt tales from Russia, Finn the Keen Falcon, Baba Yaga—who could want to read them? Rosamund.

Sometimes Cathleen thumbed through them for new stories to supplement her own store, and every so often she found what she sought, one that pleased her. But one day she came upon a fable that disturbed her deeply; and in her turn she tossed and murmured in her sleep, and woke, like Rosamund, with a scream caught in her throat.

It was a story from Yugoslavia, a brutal story, harsh and fierce like the country it came from. A poor widow, left to run the farm, had a son who loved her and worked beside her. All went well until he was twenty; and he fell in love with a girl as cruel as she was beautiful. Overnight he changed, and all things changed. His mother was nothing, the farm was nothing, all that he cared for was his sweetheart with the angel's face and savage heart. Week by week she stripped the farm of all its yield. When the old woman chided, her son smacked her across the mouth. Grimly then she did the farm work alone, and waited for the day when the spell would be broken, and the witch would lose her power over him. Week by week she saw him grow more distracted, as he strove to satisfy whims beyond all reason; and she suffered for his suffering. Then one day the girl asked for one more gift, one only; that given, she would be his bride. And the gift that she asked was his mother's heart.

He did not hesitate. Bewitched, he ran through the trees to the house, and seized a knife. When his mother looked up from her work to welcome him he ran her through. He cut through the withered flesh and scooped out her heart, still pulsing. He cradled it in the casket his sweetheart had given him, and turned to run through the dark groves to claim her. The deed was done, he had proved himself worthy of her love. But in his haste to reach his goal, he stumbled over a tree-root, and almost fell.

Then from the dripping casket a voice called his name. "Take care my son. Take care not to trip, you will hurt yourself."

Cathleen was shivering. With a thump she put the book down. Was it always like that, then? Did children care so little, and mothers so desperately? Some do, she supposed. Some don't. It was a chilling story. And I, what would I say? Would I say take care my daughter, guard your heedless feet. With great sadness she knew that she would. Not because she valued herself at nothing. But because she would be helpless: there would be nothing else she could do.

"Where's my book?" cried her daughter, pushing past her. "I need my book, I have to have it now. My book with the black cover."

"I put it down somewhere," lied Cathleen. Too grisly for a child of ten, these monstrous fables.

"I want it!" bellowed Rosamund. "You took it, I know you did. They were the best ones of all, I've got to find them."

"I don't really understand why you read fairy-tales over and over," said Cathleen, to divert her attention. "They're just the same thing over and over, in different guise."

"That's what I like," said Rosamund. She stood deliberating, then came to terms with the fact that the book had passed from her keeping. "I'll just keep looking till I find it."

Cathleen took a breath, and lied again. "I'm very sorry, Rosamund, but I burned it by mistake when I was making a bonfire with the leaves."

Rosamund measured her mother with her raking gaze. Surprisingly, she did not join battle. "It doesn't matter, I know them all by heart. I just wanted to paint a picture of one of them."

Which one it was they both knew. But by mutual consent the subject was dropped. Cathleen thought of burning the book, to give some credence to her lie: she hated lies almost as much as cruelty. Instead she asked the librarian to withdraw it from circulation. So Rosamund had to find herself a new set of nightmares.

Strange child, she never referred to the story again: perhaps, in her deepest recesses, she was glad to have it taken away. She turned away from her books, as she often did, to play with her black dolls, who had grown to a family of three, the last comer a one-armed discard from Florence. Predictably, that one was Rosamund's favourite. She fed them and clothed them and bossed them and mothered them, gave them piano lessons, used them as models for her drawings. The other girls were done with dolls, but Rosamund continued.

"They'd be sad to be given away," she told Cathleen.

"But what about the time when you're really and truly too old for them? You won't be playing with them when you're twelve, will you."

"Oh I'll put them away then for my own children. They won't mind being put away then."

"I see," said Cathleen.

Rosamund was always drawing, on paper, with a stick in the dirt, with her finger-tips against a misted window-pane. Always feeling, rubbing her hands along the underside of a leaf, brushing a dandelion clock along her cheek. Always watching: the dew on a spider's web, the curious structure of a case-moth, the way a curled-up leaf held the rain. She was clever and stupid by turn, dreamy, stubborn, often insolent. She clung close to Cathleen, chattering, then she was suddenly cocooned in her own silence. Cathleen adored her, admired her, and often found her alien.

Too busy to think of men, Cathleen found that nevertheless she had a suitor. It had occurred to her from time to time that she was foolish to refuse the overtures of interest, even affection, that came her way. Now this was one that she could not avoid, a suitor ready made through the most potent and ubiquitous force of all: propinquity.

It was a widower, a headmaster from a neighbouring school who lived in Cabbage Tree, whose children she had taught. The pleasant nuclear family of television, you would have said: husband, wife; boy, girl; money enough; one dog, one cat; everything pat. But one day when the wife drove down the hill the brakes failed, and their little shell of world exploded. As he came out of shock his eyes lighted on Cathleen, surely and unmistakably. The teachers teased her, and she blushed. His children, shy and strawberry blond like their mother, reached out to her store of compassion. He was a good man, Cathleen was sure. But she suspected that he was parsimonious—and his bulldog looks made her flesh creep. The thought of his embraces was a burden not to be borne. She hedged, pitying the children, pitying his loneliness. It was depressing to be singled out by a man she could never in a million years think of marrying. Someone else more unselfish, more sensible, less romantic would have to take on the job. Having loved once—whatever calamity waited at the end—she could settle now for nothing less. It was a relief when the year ended and she found herself transferred to Alcheringa.

7

At thirty, Cathleen was thin and somewhat sallow, no longer the nut-brown girl with rose flushing her tan, but still possessed of a gentle prettiness. She tired easily, too easily. She was glad that she no longer had to catch the bus; her new school was the old stone school refurbished and expanded, one relic of the old farming village that had survived; it was only five minutes walk from her house by the bay. She was surprised to find the children so different from those at Cabbage Tree, only five miles away. Of course in many ways all children are the same, but these new pupils were more homogeneous, less countrified, more sophisticated. A richer area, with the houses, on the whole, more palatial. The old places like her own were a minority in the township, more and more of them were being demolished and replaced by blocks of home-units.

Nothing stays the same, thought Cathleen, settling in to her new school. She was glad that she had her teaching skills tucked comfortably away, to be drawn on at will; here the mistress was young and assertive, one of the new breed of liberated young women. Next to her Cathleen felt herself a nonentity.

As for Rosamund, the change was all joy. She was in the same class as her beloved Florence, accepted without demur in the group that Florence ruled over. They were the crème de la crème de la crème of the school, the prettiest, the cleverest, the snootiest, the most with-it. They all dressed alike, in the same uniforms, the same brand of shoes, with long white socks in the same thick ribbing, the same slave-bracelets. For once Rosamund went quietly: she embraced conformity with open arms. By now, at almost twelve, she was taller than her mother, obnoxiously sure that she knew everything in the world worth knowing. When Cathleen tried to read Shakespeare to her (by the fireside, out on the garden-swing) she put her hands over her ears. When Cathleen tried to teach her the piano, she slammed out horrible discords.

"I don't understand you," said Cathleen helplessly. "You used to like poetry. You were playing the piano so well."

"I hate poetry!" yelled Rosamund. "I liked it when I was a kid! I don't want to have my mother teaching me music. You're not my BRAIN! I want to learn from Mr. Beaver. All the girls do. He's fabulous!"

So Rosamund learned from the fabulous Mr. Beaver. It was their second real clash, and this time Rosamund was victorious. I guess it will always be like that now, she is stronger than I am, and ruthless like her father, thought Cathleen, opening the door to the new music-master, a ladylike little gentleman who rolled his eyes and went into transports of delight while he played Rustle of Spring.

"It's very banal, the music that he plays," said Cathleen waspishly. "Very hackneyed."

"I like it," said Rosamund.

Waste of time, his lessons. Cathleen was cross whenever she heard the imprecision of both teacher and pupil. One memorable day Rosamund called her into the sitting room.

"Come quickly, mum. There's a horrible smell in this room. There's a dead mouse in the piano, I think."

Indeed there was a horrible smell. The perpetrator stood cornered and blushing, wringing his hands in embarrassment and distress; meanwhile Rosamund stood on the piano stool and dragged at the top of the piano, determined to nose the culprit out.

Cathleen wanted to scream with rude laughter. That graveyard smell—what on earth had the poor little man been eating?—that crazy possessed child—

She forced herself to speak calmly. "Please don't make a fuss, Rosamund. Look, it's almost gone now! I said, don't fuss, did you hear me? We'll get the—the mouse out later, after your lesson. Please sit down, Mr. Beaver, and play us—um—the Waltz of the Flowers—"

But Mr. Beaver remembered that he had another appointment, and that he must be toddling along.

When he had gone, Cathleen enlightened Rosamund, but she still refused to believe. A search of the piano's innards disclosed no shred of mouse, not even a decaying apple-core.

"I think it was you, then," said Rosamund, finally. "And you just put the blame on poor Mr. Beaver."

How wilful she is and how full of caprice, thought Cathleen. I have been too soft with her, leaned too far backwards to see that her needs were always met: I have negated my own personality for hers. Yet, perhaps, she thought with sudden fear, the truth is that I have no personality at all. I was my parents' child, and Brian's bedfellow, and my child's mother. There is no me left at all: perhaps there never was one. I was so busy being a good little girl, pleasing my parents, the apple of their eyes, and glad of it, manipulated by them as Rosamund manipulates her black dolls; and somewhere in the process the spark that distinguishes me got put out. Always supposing that I had one. She gave a bleak little smile at the sight of herself succumbing to the fashionable disease of blaming parents for whatever went wrong. You a homosexual? Blame it on your mother. A hoodlum? It's all dad's doing. There was something in what they said, no doubt; always a grain of truth, or even a dollop in the sweeping manifestos of the young, but for all that, dear Brutus—Well, I was always an underling by nature, a mirror, a shadow.

But Rosamund, she was substance, and while Cathleen deplored her unruly girl, so full of shenanigans, glowering one moment and boisterously gay the next, still she rejoiced in her. So tall, so comely, a daughter of the gods, really, larger than life. Each day brought forth its tempests, with floods of tears and exuberant calms to follow.

Seeing her child change to maiden, Cathleen nerved herself to speak of menstruation. Shy as her mother before her had been, she chose a quiet moment (few and far-between these, with a house swarming with girls) to proffer a book.

"You're growing up so fast, darling. I daresay you'll need to know about all the changes in your—well, in your body. This book sets it all out clearly, much better than I could. If you read it, then you can ask me about anything that puzzles you."

Rosamund made no attempt to take the book. "That old stuff, I've known all about that for donkey's years."

Winded, Cathleen strove to conceal it. "Oh! Who told you?"

"Patsy, of course. Ages ago, when we were about ten, or something. She took us down to the tool-shed to see her dog with the dog next door. She used to tell us all about the curse and sex and all that stuff when we had our pyjama parties."

So that was the meaning of the muffled hoots and giggles that went on long past midnight. Dogs indeed! Cathleen spoke angrily. "That pernicious child! I knew I shouldn't have let you

63

play with her. And from now on I won't."

"You can't stop me," said Rosamund.

How true! Angrier still, Cathleen raised her voice as she so
rarely did. "I always hated that know-it-all smirk on her face.
And that greasy note in her voice."

"Well, we all thought she was super, knowing all that stuff.
She used to spy on her mother kissing Uncle Freddy through a
hole in the wall-boards."

Cathleen was silent. She had always mistrusted the tall skinny
world-weary girl (world-weary at thirteen, yet) a year older than
the others in her class, but a world older in wakeupness. On the
make. Gutsy, yes, and loyal to that terrible family of hers, but
so patently, so blatantly out for herself. Whenever she came to
stay the night she used every skerrick of hot water to shampoo
her hair, used Cathleen's French talcum powder, wheedled all
manner of things out of Rosamund. She lived with her mother
and her three brothers in a near-dump between Alcheringa and
Cabbage Tree, surrounded by rusty bits of the cars from the
wrecks that the boys were forever demolishing. Their father had
flown the coop long years before, and one uncle succeeded
another in Patsy's life.

"Like her cheek! Taking it on herself to enlighten you."
Actually, now that she was over her indignation, Cathleen was
rather relieved. For in spite of her cheek and grabbiness, there
was something clean-cut and true about Patsy. Rosamund
could have gone farther for an instructor and fared worse.

"I thought it sounded stupid," said Rosamund, sprawled now
upon her belly, drawing swags of roses on her homework book.
"So did Liz. But Sara and Flo thought it was a nifty way of
doing things."

"It's the way Nature arranged it." Cathleen's lips twitched.
"You'll all cope when the time comes."

Rosamund had lost interest. "Can I join the swimming club?
All the other kids are. Not Patsy," she added craftily. "Jenny's
father's getting it going down at the rock pool on Saturdays,
we'll have a club costume and badges and all that, Jenny says.
You can come and teach the little kids to swim, if you like."

"Thank you," Cathleen answered. "But I get more than
enough of teaching little kids through the week. If they're
desperate for help I'll come. Otherwise I'll stay at home and

catch up on my schoolwork and do some pruning."

Jumbo had died, suddenly, and, so it seemed, easily, as he snoozed on the verandah. Rosamund grieved for him: when she gave her love she gave it without reserve. She made an elaborate cairn of stones for his tomb, and planted trailing rosemary between the crevices. "I love you, Jumbo." she wrote on a wooden slat, and buried it with him, together with the rubber ball he guarded and growled over, even when he was too old to chase it. Her tears wet his little grizzled face as she kissed him goodbye. With cheeks still tear-wet she turned from his grave to watch three tiny lizards sunning themselves on a brick.

"Look, mum, quick, look!" she called. "They make a pattern like a Greek key—No, you're too late, they've gone." Now she was smiling, capricious child.

Capricious child, sentimental girl, which was it? Both. Neither. From moment to moment she changed. When Cathleen brought her a new pup from the pound, she refused at first to look at it. From then on she refused to be parted from it; at night it lay on the rug beside her bed. She decided to name the little black kelpie Bess, after her favourite heroine of the moment, the highwayman's sweetheart.

She was beginning to reject the clothes that her mother bought for her. "Pink and white checks again!"—she groaned. "Oh mum, I like plain clothes. I hate pink, it *stinks*."

She was very pleased with the navy-blue swimsuits that were chosen for the swimming club. Sleek and unencumbered they looked, the five girls; or at least until they donned the shapeless tracksuits that had also been chosen.

"Those horrible bulky things," grumbled Cathleen. "You look like a boy, not a girl, Rosamund."

"Wanna bet?" asked bold Rosamund, and all the girls giggled.

"Well, you would if I'd been misguided enough to let you get your hair cut." Cathleen chose to ignore the innuendo. A good way to discover boys, under the auspices of the sporty salty crew who ran the club.

"Yes, why can't I get my hair cut. I can't get a bathing-cap big enough to squash it inside. Everyone else has short hair. Why have I got to have all this stuff like rope?"

"Your hair's pretty, Rosie," said Sara, scratching her own

curly dark shingle.

"It's Swedish," said Florence, and that settled it. "My father says so."

Cathleen was grateful to Florence for her support. "Yes, she does look Swedish with those broad shoulders and golden hair. It must come from a long way back. Really, Rosamund, with your strong features you need all the hair you can get."

That set them all laughing. They chuckled so much that they nearly choked on the plums they were eating, a colander full from the tree outside the kitchen window.

"That sounds a funny thing to need. Hair," said Liz.

"Rapunzel didn't think so," Cathleen reminded them. "When she let her hair down for the prince to climb up."

"Oh, is that what you need it for?" asked Sara, always literal.

"Samson should have hung onto his," said Cass.

They laughed again, the ring of pretty blossoming girls, poised so delicately on this moment of time, childhood still clinging to them as the dew clings to the butterfly emerging from the chrysalis. One moment, then the wings are dried, are spread in flight. Bright-eyed, juice dripping through their fingers, they leaned together, remembering their days in the cocoon.

"Remember when we used to keep silkworms, Mrs. Bell? And we were forever pestering you for mulberry leaves?"

"They felt cool, those silkworms. Their bodies were like satin. Or silk," said Rosamund.

"That's why they're called silkworms," said Sara.

"No, it isn't!" Squabbling, jostling, laughing, they went in to get their towels. "Bye," they called, as they took off for the club.

There were five of them left now, always together: Rosie, Flo, Sara, Liz, Cass. Sometimes Patsy joined them, and that was the signal for squabbles. She could twist them around those skinny fingers, covered with cheap rings and warts, hold them enthralled with her talk of boys and discothèques and horse-shows. She had dredged up a rich crony from Lord knows where, and so had little time to spend with her old friends. Cathleen was glad.

The girls who could not resist her (so sophisticated, they said) were not displeased to see her go. They congregated in each house by turn, but mostly in Florence's because of its opulence, or Rosamund's, because there they could do as they pleased. If they wanted to take sleeping bags outside to spend the night with the mosquitoes on the lawn, or to play records until near-dawn, there was no father to bellow out that he needed his sleep, and for God's sake turn that bloody thing off. As fathers always do, Rosamund reported, all fathers. Together they played tennis. Together they skated in the barn four suburbs distant. They learned to water-ski. They went sailing in Florence's Mirror, with its red sails. At weekends the bay was dotted with small craft, sails of all colours. To see them returning, with the setting sun at their backs, to see the evening mists come up behind the slow-coaches, never failed to delight Cathleen. She blessed the good luck that had guided her to this sequestered plot.

Together, in a platoon, looking quite small and frightened, the girls put on their new school uniforms and took the plunge into a new world: high school. Cathleen, busy with her own class, managed to get two hours off to take her Rosamund across. Her heart yearned towards her daughter, outwardly so calm, but clenching her fists so that she would not start biting her nails again. From the big wheels of primary school they had been reduced to the most insignificant of cogs. The older children shoved them aside as they waited in the lines at canteen.

At first they hated it. Then suddenly they found it fun. It was groovy to have half a dozen different teachers. They all professed themselves in love with the young Science master; they all hated the English mistress. In short they had found their feet. Within a term they considered themselves the élite of first form. They wore tortoiseshell slides in their hair, spiced their conversation with cosmopolitan (they thought) exclamations, like Ma foie! or Merde! and affected an air of languor. Summoned to the headmaster's office for smoking at the back of the bus—well, hardly smoking, one cigarette between five— they agreed to weep at a certain signal. Together, in a body, they were pardoned.

"Will you keep your promise not to smoke again?" asked Cathleen, disturbed.

"Of course we will. We weren't really smoking, anyway, just pretending to annoy that stuck-up Robin Frobisher. She thinks she owns the stinking bus, because she's a prefect."

They whispered together, the five of them; they invented code-words of their own. They brought out a short-lived publication, The Daily Cad. They rarely consented to accompany their parents anywhere. Only with the greatest difficulty, as they entered their teens, could they be coaxed into allowing mothers to participate in the buying of their clothes; and that only because their mothers held the purse-strings.

Rosamund dug in her heels: no way now would she learn the piano. They all refused to keep on with their piano lessons. Mr. Beaver was bewildered. What had he done to offend them? Not a thing; it was just that he was old hat. Five of them, as one girl had decided to learn folk guitar—Five mothers went quietly. Four of the guitars were exactly the same, but Rosamund's was shaped like a lute. It sounded the same, or near enough, but it had a belly like a calabash.

"Trust Rosie!" they sighed. They wished that theirs were fat-bellied, too. But their mothers were meanies, and closed their purses tight.

Under the grape-vine, under the fig tree, behind the honeysuckle-hedge, they lolled about, plucking the strings and singing mournful ballads. Rosamund's voice was sweet and husky, Sara's sweet and high. But Florence, a clown like her father, was almost tone-deaf, and she made noises like a bullfrog until they chucked fallen figs at her, and shouted at her to be quiet.

They were all crazy about the Beatles. Harassed, Cathleen gave permission for Rosamund to join the others at the rort at the Stadium where their idols were performing.

"You're such a sheep, Rosamund," she accused her child. "All you do these days is copy the others. Once you had some individuality. Do you remember how you used to get up at daybreak to pick mushrooms. Now you're terrified to even think for yourself."

Rosamund didn't care about being called names, as long as she was allowed to have her way. "Can I go then?" she asked, determined to be a sheep if sheep were the name of the game.

Cathleen nodded. But when the battle of the discos came up she stood firm. All the mothers stood firm. They telephoned one another for reassurance, but not one broke ranks, none of the five girls set foot in a discothèque that year.

"Can I go skiing then?" Rosamund was going to drive some kind of a bargain. At thirteen and a half she was selfish and ruthless, beginning to feel her power over boys, over life. Notes were brought out folded from her blazer pocket, to be exhibited to her friends. All five had notes to be exhibited. From matinées at the picture show they had graduated to the four o'clock pash sessions. Next summer, they said, they were leaving the swimming club and getting bikinis.

So it seems, thought Cathleen, that this winter will be the last vacation that I will spend with my child. She capitulated suddenly. She could afford a holiday. She needed a holiday.

"We'll all go skiing," she said. "Find out which girls can come, and I'll take you in the August vacation. That's if the snows hold."

Five of them, six, counting the duenna, took the train to a whole other life. Only Florence had ever seen snow before. They drove from Cooma into a white and improbable world.

"I think it's fairyland," said Rosamund solemnly. "It's like all the fairy-tales I used to read when I was a kid. Thanks for bringing us, mum."

"Thank you," the others echoed, dutifully.

What fun it was, how cold! How their cheeks stung, and their noses were roses!

To her surprise, Cathleen found that she was quite good, quicker to learn than the girls. Soon she was promoted to the class of the so-tanned Austrian instructor, who plied her with extra lessons. Woman-chaser, she thought, as his eyes met hers. He was rubbing her knee with snow to dissipate a bruise, or so he said. She had forgotten how pleasant it was to be caressed, even in this cursory and public fashion. It was heady to encounter his frank recognition of her as a woman.

"You have beautiful balance," he said, unleashing his white teeth in a smile. "It is hard to believe that you have never skied before."

Short of a bed-mate, I suppose, since the last lot moved on, she thought dryly. Yet she smiled back at him, flattered.

"Mum!" yelled Rosamund. "We need you over here. Quick."

"Excuse me," said Cathleen, with finality, and went to do her daughter's bidding. The next day she saw him rubbing somebody else's knee. So! So what!

8

The years, it seems, gather momentum as they roll. Or so it appeared to Cathleen, picking the last of the daffodils when they came home from the snowfields. Could it truly be four months since she had planted them? It seemed four weeks. No sooner had the liquidambar burst its cerements and stood green-mantled than it flamed red and purple; winced under wind's onslaught; stood naked under a wintry moon. She found that she was sweeping up the autumn leaves before she had begun to gaze her fill.

She was a good teacher, calm and competent, soft-spoken but firm, loving but detached. Once or twice she came close to caring too much for a child. A little aboriginal boy, wild as a young dingo, with strange light eyes and the tenderest hands she had ever seen. Once in a while he came to play with her dogs, the two of them. Bess had been joined by Billy, a waif who moved with panache from the school garbage-bins to a berth at the end of Cathleen's bed.

"I like them dogs," he told Cathleen. "When I go back to the farm I got six dogs there."

The young couple who had adopted him, doted on him. They were nomads, all three of them, only perching in Alcheringa for a few weeks before they went back to their commune. No wonder they love him, thought Cathleen, so would I. What would it be like to have a son, to be custodian of all that male bravado? I wish I knew, she thought with a pang. In her bones she felt that she would never know.

It was absurd really that each day left her so wrung-out. The children she dealt with were on the whole, children of privilege, blessed denizens of this tropical garden between two waters, sea crashing against the eastern shores, still water lapping the west. Her work was engrossing but not exhausting. She could only suppose she had few reserves to draw on, and that as she grew older they were increasingly depleted. What energies she had left at the end of each day she husbanded for her daughter, who often repulsed her, yet seemed to need her to be there, fit target.

Rosamund and her friends had graduated from folk guitar to flamenco. They toyed with the idea of forming a flamenco group to travel the world to collect a great deal of money and fame. Their flamenco teacher, a boy as dark as he was aquiline, was the reason for their change of heart. He came to the house sometimes, and after the girls had stumbled through their simple sevillanas, he played the strange rhythms of the malaguenas and granadinas, while they listened, rapt.

All the girls swooned over him. Which one would he choose?

"You're wasting your time," said Cathleen. "All he really cares about, girls, is his guitar and his audience. You don't stand a chance."

"Oh, horrible Mrs. Bell! You old wet blanket," they moaned.

"We know he has to fall in love with one of us. We're irresistible," said Florence, only half joking.

"What would you do if by some strange chance that did happen? If he did single one of you out? Would you murder her? Or tar and feather her?"

"No, we made a pact," they said earnestly.

It was very seductive: the summer night with the soft lap, lap of the bay at the bottom of the garden, with the moonflowers opening, and over all the fiery cascades of music unloosed by his fingers. All that summer the girls were draped against trees, on swings, on the lawn, listening.

In vain the boys with zinc on their peeling noses called to take them to the beach, or to barbecues. They had better things to do.

Dark-eyed, long-fingered, he played on their awakening senses. He was Hungarian, they whispered. No, wait, his father was Hungarian. Or was he Spanish? His mother was a gypsy, Sara knew it for a fact. He spoke French like a native. He was the older man they had all dreamed of. He was nineteen.

All the surfing boys hated him. When would he be going back to Hungary, they asked. Soon? Like tomorrow? Rosamund's superseded cavalier, a stripling of sixteen, said that he was sick of going to parties by himself. He wasn't going to hang around forever. Rosamund shrugged. They all shrugged.

Sara had somehow discovered, she knew it for a fact she said, that Tamas's father owned an art gallery somewhere in Sydney. An *art gallery*? Feverishly Rosamund started painting again. Perhaps he would sit for her: in a romantic pose, like the young man with the flowers in Hilliard's portrait? Perhaps, he said.

71

The other girls hated her; because she was using it to cheat. One day he seemed to prefer one, the next day another. Soon, he said, he would go to Spain, to continue his study of flamenco. It had to be Spain, he explained, gravely, flamenco is a domestic art. They nodded sagely: how wise he was.

All in all, it would be a relief when he went. The girls were starting to squabble about him. Patsy had appeared from nowhere, complete with guitar, to vie for his attention.

"Patsy thinks she's sexy," they hissed. But they were too frightened or mesmerised to send her away.

The boy, Tamas, did not appear to find her attractive. Actually, Cathleen realised, he's probably more taken with me than with any of them. He's the sort of lad who would naturally gravitate towards an older woman. Perhaps when he goes abroad he'll find one for himself. She allowed herself a moment's pleasant fantasy as her eyes rested on the boy, such a lean brown body, such a beautiful face.—Meeting her gaze, he smiled at her, and she smiled back, lowering her eyes. When she looked up Rosamund stood between them, glaring at her, menacing her with the daggers of her gaze, reminding her that she was a mother, and old as well.

When he took ship to Spain and left them sighing, they all gave up the guitar. In six houses six guitars lay in their cases, unplucked.

One day Gert Levy telephoned Cathleen with a query. "Look, Cathy, I think I'll have to go quietly about these damn discos. If Tony calls for them afterwards—say about eleven—or eleven thirty—which do you think?—"

"Eleven," said Cathleen.

"Will you let Rosie go, then?"

"I suppose so," said Cathleen.

The discothèque fad did not last long, however: three months from beginning to end. The smoky air and the guttering candles, the throbbing and sexual beat of the music, all delighted the newcomers. The boys who asked them to dance were different, rough-spoken but self-reliant. Or so Cathleen gathered from the snippets of conversation, broken off abruptly when she came into the room. Dutifully they turned up at the disco every week, as they had turned up at Sunday school six, seven, years before. Within a month they had outgrown their rendezvous, but refused to admit that they were bored.

Sara was the first to throw in the towel. "Half of the boys there," she grumbled, "they're only pimply goons still at school, even if it's not our school, they're still schoolkids, and they've still got pimples."

Liz joined in. "The other half are apprentices and beach layabouts, all they want to do is to find any girl at all to sit in their beat-up cars to be pawed."

"If only they weren't so ugly," Cass lamented.

"Or so gross. That fat little thing with a face like a Toby jug wiped his sweaty hands down the back of my new white dress," said Rosamund.

They saw Cathleen tying up the wisteria that had fallen down from the pergola, but they did not lower their voices. In other words, the discos had had their day.

9

Each year, thought Cathleen, with infinite sadness, my child grows farther away from me, rejects me more, shuts me outside, replaces me. Was it for this I struggled all those years heaving that vast old woman around, making a living for us, giving up chances that—who knows—might have led somewhere. Where has she gone, my dear little girl?

Everything was different now. They were chalk and cheese. Cathleen tried to remember her own time of adolescence, wondering whether she had been so secretive and jealous and had conveniently chosen to forget. She was sure she hadn't. When her mother left the square packet of pads on her dressing-table, each month, without comment, she was pleased. Relieved that there was no comment, even more relieved that she was spared the task of going into a chemist's shop, and unthinkably, asking the chemist. Yet now when she tried to do the same office for Rosamund, she was confronted by a virago.

"Don't you ever dare to embarrass me in front of my friends again!" She was eating a meat pie: she had just come in from riding her bicycle down to the cake shop. She was always starving.

"What did I do?" asked Cathleen, bewildered.

"Don't pretend you don't know. Just before we went out! You put that horrible packet down on my bed in front of Patsy. As if I was a baby! Now she'll go and make fun of me!"

"But Rosamund, you're being absurd. It's a natural process. Patsy herself—"

"Not because of that! I hate it because you treat me like a baby. Patsy's mother doesn't buy them for her, none of the mothers do—"

"Oh, be quiet!" said Cathleen, stung, as she seldom was, to a sharp retort. "You're too ungrateful."

She was unprepared for the fury who launched herself across the room. She staggered backwards before the force of her big strong girl, who was, suddenly, unmercifully, grinding a meat-pie into her face.

By the time she had recovered the door had banged behind her attacker. Slowly she clawed the spicy meat from her face,

74

and went into the bathroom to finish cleaning herself off. So this was the end of it, all the suffering and struggling. She burst into tears and her tears mingled with the debris on her cheeks.

At dusk Rosamund came back still mutinous, and—actually—aggrieved.

"Send me to boarding-school if you like," she shrugged. "I don't care. I hate it here, anyway."

"Why do you hate it?"

"Oh, it's all so cloistered! I'm mummy's little girl. You live such a sheltered life. There isn't even anyone else in the family. It's all so *twee.*"

"I can't help that." Cathleen was aggrieved, also. "I'd have liked it much better if I'd had a husband and other children, too. I hate having all my eggs in one basket!" She began to cry, harsh sobs that racked her throat. She had not cried, really cried for fifteen years, since she had parted from Brian. "You're like your father!" she cried out. "Selfish and cruel!"

Rosamund came a step closer. "Who is my father?" she demanded. "I've got a right to know. Not just that soft soap you've been handing me about how he died when I was a baby, sob, sob. The truth! I've got a right to know the truth."

Cathleen faced her. "I've told you as much as it's good for you to know."

"Tell me the truth!" Rosamund's eyes stared, burned. She was as adamant as a judge.

Judge me then, thought Cathleen. If you are to be my enemy, why then should I protect you? There's nothing worse that you can do to me, nothing that can make you look at me with eyes more filled with hatred. Or scorn.

"Are you old enough to know?" she asked. "Are you sure?"

Rosamund nodded. The only sound in the room was her breathing.

"He's a painter. You've heard of him. Brian Clancy." So it was all said.

"Clancy? My father?"

Cathleen could not look at her. She stared down at a scratch on the table, shaped like a dart. "We were never married," she said, very low. "He took me away with him when my mother died. But I wanted to go. When I knew I was going to have a baby I thought he'd want to marry me. But he didn't." After a moment she forced herself to look up, to meet the blue gaze of her cruel lover's cruel daughter. To her amazement she saw those eyes were brimming, and the cleft chin, so like her father's, was trembling.

"Poor old ma," said Rosamund. "So you had to make it all by yourself. Do you know, I reckon you've done a pretty good job."

I'll never understand her, never, thought Cathleen. When I try to help her she scorns me. When I tell her what must invite her scorn she looks at me with love.

Rosamund's voice was quite thick. She took a step, bent down, and brushed her lips against her mother's cheek.

And she burst out laughing, Irish child, chameleon. "You taste like a pie, mum," she chuckled. "Why didn't you eat it? It's not like you to be so wasteful."

Cathleen still had one question to ask. "Don't you mind? Rosamund?"

"Mind! I think it's super. It's all so romantic. And he's a very good painter, too, even though he does copy from Bosch."

"He was a weakling," said Cathleen sternly. "He told me to have an abortion, and then he ran away."

"So he doesn't know about me at all?" Rosamund stood still, listening to some voice of her own.

Cathleen shook her head. "Nobody knows—or knew. I was alone in the world. It's a long story. Some day I'll tell you."

"Oh it doesn't matter," said Rosamund cheerfully. "I know everything I need to know, really. It's all pretty exciting, I think. Not just like any old father at all. Some day I'll go looking for him."

And leave me, thought Cathleen, forlorn. And show yourself as inescapably his child. Peacocks both of you, two of a kind, and I am the pea-hen, the colour of mud.

Rosamund, sensitive as her father had never allowed himself to be, read her thoughts. "But I'll never forget how you had the guts to go it alone, mum. And I'm glad you did have me, in spite of what he said. Think what I'd have missed out on! Living!"

She turned away, having said more perhaps than she had meant to. She went into her room whistling the fragment of song that was always on her lips. In a moment, the voice of

Melba, pure and urgent, took over the aubade. Rosamund was on a Melba kick that year.

10

Often, too often, in the times that followed, Cathleen held fast to those words. Sometimes she thought that she must have imagined them: fifteen to seventeen is almost as bad as thirteen to fifteen: different, but still bad. Still, they had been spoken, those words of love and trust; once said they could never be unsaid.

And since time and the hour do run through the roughest day, the scenes and tantrums did at last begin to space themselves out. Rosamund had replaced the knot of friends by a charming shy boy with a stammer. Since his mother, divorced, had taken herself a new young husband, who kept her moving at a swift pace, she had little time to spend with her two boys. One of them, the younger, didn't care. This one, Johnny, hated being ousted.

Because he was falling behind in his school work, Rosamund delved into her capacious stores of pity and bossiness. It was the black dolls all over again. She made soup for him and watched him play football on Saturdays, helped him with his maths and English on Sundays, He was very lazy, but with her strong will she steered him through his examinations. Fourth year over, he left school and was apprenticed to a plumber. For a while they continued to meet, but without their daily contact it soon became clear that there was no common ground. Their fugitive kisses had not led them into deeper tanglewood, so it all ended easily and amicably.

The girls were back, this time with boys in tow. For Rosamund there was a boy not long out from Sweden, not at all handsome, but with immense charm. He had a memorable face and a tall disjointed body like a stick insect's, which he used with extraordinary suppleness. Nils, he was called.

"You have such charisma," Cathleen told him. "Whenever you come in, things start happening."

"Darling Mrs. Bell," he murmured, accepting his due. Really, he already spoke all the English he would ever need to know. "But Rosie is like that too, don't you think? I heard a very old song the other day about a girl called Lulu who bursted up every party she went to—"

"Oh, I know that song. My father loved it. He used to play it on an old wind-up gramophone he had." She stopped short, remembering.

"Where is it now, that gramophone?" asked Nils. "I want to hear it—" Cathleen shook her head. Where was it? Given away, or thrown away. She had never gone back to ask. She forced herself back to the present.

Nils was jigging around, improvising a sort of turkey trot, singing bits of the song in a weird falsetto. Cathleen joined in. She knew the words off by heart, and sang them through; until Nils seized her and forced her to do a Charleston at his side. Puffed out, laughing, they finally ran themselves to a stop.

"Whenever you're ready, Nils." There was Rosamund, clothed in purple from head to toe, a hooded caftan it was, embroidered in what looked like white swastikas. She was all ready for their jaunt into town, and not at all pleased to see her mother kicking up her heels. "We'll miss the bus."

Nils bowed low, clicking his heels. He was always acting a part. "At your service, gnädige Frau," he said. "Don't forget, Mrs. Bell. Save me the waltz." Nils and Rosamund were currently crazy about the twenties.

Nils and Rosamund were crazy, full stop. They had both decided that they were going to direct films, and they haunted the way-out movie houses.

"Nils. Come *on!*" called Rosamund, but it was too late. The bus had turned the corner, and was lumbering down the street away from them. Unless they donned seven-league boots they had no hope of catching it.

Rosamund was cross. "Thanks a lot! If you hadn't stayed drivelling to my old woman."

"Was I talking drivel, Mrs. Bell? We were perfecting an art form, Rosie."

"Oh—I'm really very annoyed with both of you. Thanks a lot," she repeated.

"I wish you wouldn't use that phrase. You know I dislike it," said Cathleen.

"That's why I said it, old woman."

"And don't call me old woman. I hate it," Cathleen retorted, nettled.

"Alright, old woman." Rosamund was going to make

someone pay for the fact that she had missed the start of a film she had been waiting all year to see. "The newest Bergman," she moaned. "Of course it had to be that one."

"Ingrid Bergman? Is she still making pictures? In my day—"

They burst out laughing. Nils remembered his manners, ran his hands over his mouth, and presented a poker face to her. "I'm sorry Mrs. Bell. I didn't mean to be rude. It's Ingmar Bergman, the director. We're always glad of a chance to see his films."

"His technique. His cutting," breathed Rosamund. "The way he intersperses word and action."

"Close-ups!" cried Nils. "Will you ever forget—"

Cathleen left them to their drooling. She liked Nils for himself, seldom had she seen a fledgling so fascinating nor one so unmistakably destined to soar. And she was grateful for the kind of company he offered Rosamund. His nonchalant lack of committal to any one person but himself amused and pleased Cathleen; he would be good for her proud daughter.

Sometimes, however, his pranks went too far. He gave Cathleen two tickets for a revival of The Decameron, urging her to take one of her Catholic friends to see it. A matchless picture of Church life in the fifteenth century, he said.

Cathleen was doubtful. "But surely the Decameron is very bawdy, Nils?"

"Oh of course if you're *chicken*," he said haughtily. "What's a little whiff of bawdiness? I thought you'd like the frescos—Giotto, you know—And the churchmen—and the nuns—"

"Thank you, Nils," said Cathleen. "I'll ask Monica Leahy."

"Do that," said Nils. "She'll love it."

The funny thing was, Miss Leahy did love it. An old schoolteacher, Catholic and sixty, she was less taken aback than Cathleen. After their first shock, the two of them didn't stop laughing.

When it was over Cathleen apologised, "I was misled by one of my daughter's friends. The one who gave me the tickets," she added.

"You should have known, Cathleen. You are very naïve my dear."

"I know," replied Cathleen humbly.

Nils didn't appear for a week. When he finally came, he made a great show of being penitent.

"Mea culpa," he said, beating his breast. "I hope you didn't mind the rude bits, Mrs. Bell."

"It was all rude bits," said Cathleen.

Now that they were in fifth form, they were all beginning to direct their thoughts towards the futures they must carve out for themselves. The girls who had gone each step of the way together elected to go to university. It would be quite easy for them all, providing that they worked steadily, and didn't get entangled with boys not committed to work at all.

Nils was different; he wanted to do something offbeat. Sometimes he talked to Cathleen about his plans, which varied from grandiose to very grandiose.

"Nils, don't you think that you'll need something else? Just while you're making it in films, of course, I mean." Cathleen added carefully. "A bread and butter job?"

"How clever you are, Mrs. Bell. Now I know where Rosie learned to be a clearvoyant." He ignored Rosamund's scowl, and prattled on. "That's exactly what I do need, a bread and butter job. I've worked it out. I'm going to learn the food and wine bit, from the bottom up."

"You mean you'll start at the bottom," said Rosamund. "And it's clairvoyant, not clearvoyant."

Nils hit his head with his fist. "Clairvoyant," he muttered. "I'll never learn this English of yours.—What was I saying. Oh yes, I'll open a joint (a joint, is that right, Rosie?) all red plush and chandeliers, and call it the Red Light. Rosie, you can work there. Beautiful waitresses in their birthday suits—Rosie taught me that yesterday—very snazzy, eh? Food of the gods—Music—"

Rosamund was convulsed. "Nils, you're quite mad! And birthday suits—well, that's a kind of a joke. You don't use that phrase in a serious context."

"And who said my eatorium is a serious place? It is strictly for rich people who want to be gay."

Rosamund was off again. "Gay," she said, braying with laughter. "Gay means—Oh Nils, I think you mean sybarites, not poofs—"

"Poofs?—Ah poofters—No need to be so detrimental—"

"Derogatory, you mean—"

"Your terrible dreadful language," said Nils. "I should have stayed in Stockholm."

Away they went, down to the stand of banana trees by the bay, where they often took their ease; as Nils remarked, it was secluded, and still close to the comforts of kitchen and lavatory.

The boys who squired Sara and Cass, Liz and Flo, were replaced from time to time, but tended, on the whole, to be rather arty.

"Hearties or arties, that's all we've got to choose from," said Sara. She had supplanted Florence as Rosamund's best friend. "We're all going to the film festival this year. Our last fling before we settle down to the grind. Why don't you come?"

Because Rosamund wouldn't like it, thought Cathleen. Aloud she said, "Thank you, Sara, but I couldn't stand the pace."

Really, only the very young could stand the devastating programme—thirty films in a dozen different languages—run off over ten days. Nils was the only one who never missed a session. Bags hung under his brown eyes, his straw-coloured hair grew more lank each day, but he got full value for his ticket. By the end of the time he was a zombie with a swelled head.

"How many did you miss?" He cathecised Sara. "Rosie missed five."

"I heard you snoring in the last one," said Rosamund.

"Lies, lies, lies."

Sara was counting up. "I think I missed eleven," Sara, thin as a biscuit, had skin blue-stained from fatigue. "I don't know how you kept it up, Nils."

"Where there's a Nils there's a way," he said, going off into spasms of laughter at his own joke.

"You know what," discovered Sara, blinking at him. "You ought to be a mime, like Marceau."

"That's often occurred to me," said Cathleen. "You just have to stand on one leg to make people want to laugh."

"Or even on two." Rosamund liked to deflate him. "Yes, why not, Nils?"

But he shook his head. "Food and films, that's all I'm interested in. But I might—I just might—get a little act ready for the school concert. You two may take part. And three other girls; and David, too, if he's very good."

"Tell us," they implored.

"Later, later, my little chickadees," he said, this time in the nasal tones of W.C. Fields.

At last Cathleen was permitted to watch the dress-rehearsal of Nils' tableaux, as he was pleased to call them. She had heard the hoots and shouts of mirth from the strip of lawn, where the garden ran into the bay. She had seen Rosamund sawing at packing cases and painting sheets of black cardboard, had seen Sara draping herself in curtains she had dyed vermilion. David, who was trying to get into N.I.D.A. was doing some sort of commentary; his rich (too rich?) modulated voice came to her ears as she sat on the verandah, sewing costumes for her own school play. She had seen Billy's feathery tail frisking (had they roped him in too?), had seen naked legs, half-naked bodies, flitting in and out behind the banana fronds. What were they up to? Wait, they commanded, for the rehearsal.

The moment came. At dusk, with the lights coming out in the dark semi-circle of hill across the water, Cathleen was escorted down to her place of honour on a knoll, by David. He was rather shy because he said she might find the tableaux offensive.

"Are they connected with sex?" Cathleen asked gravely, suppressing a laugh.

"Very," he said, and made off.

Cathleen spread her skirts around her, and hugged her knees. Six small separate scenes had been set up, side by side, rather like the houses in Season at Sarsaparilla. Presumably they would each be lit up in turn.

The scufflings grew less. David intoned:—

"In this country both carnal and callous,
No perversion's regarded with malice,
And each lady is willing,
To make a quick shilling—

(Deep bow)—Be our guest at the court of King Phallus."

The hessian curtain of the first box was ripped back. There, beneath branches from the fig tree, with a fig leaf over flesh-coloured trunks lay Nils, with his arm around Sara, also in flesh coloured tights. In a parody of desire he was kissing her arm, gnawing it, really, from finger-tips to shoulder, while she rolled her eyes at him, and David intoned again, plummily.

"In the garden of Eden lay Adam,

83

Contentedly fondling his madam,
And great was his mirth
For in all the wide earth
There were only two balls—and he had 'em."

When he came to the punch line Nils pushed his Eve aside and sprang to his feet. In his hands were two yellow balls. Frantically he began to juggle them. They fell, he chased them. Feverishly, on his knees, he tossed them up, dropped them, crawled in pursuit. The light went off. Curtain.

The next tableau had Rosamund as a pretty young lass with a truly magnificent ass. Her rounded behind, encased in pink fishnet, was presented to the audience of one. The ass that charged out to bunt her in the buttocks as she rose in surprise was half Florence, half Florence's Jim.

"Angelina's a pretty young lass
With a truly magnificent ass
Not dimpled and pink
As you probably think
But it's grey, has long ears, and eats grass."

Curtain. Behind the scenes there was a sound of breaking and someone called out Shit. Someone else called Keep it clean! David, rather ruffled, stepped out to announce that the chamber-pot had broken, and that the priest's vestments had somehow been left behind.

"Our performance must of necessity be curtailed" he said pompously. "This must be our final offering of the night." He began—

"Have you heard about Magda Lupescu
Who came to Rumania's rescue?—"

The curtain, ripped back one too many times, ripped in two. No matter. There was Nils, in a red wig and a gauzy nightgown, with rhinestone earrings, reclining beneath a dummy king complete with cardboard crown. He stretched out his arms, simpering, ogling. But—David had forgotten his lines—Panic. His mouth opened and shut. But Nils was there.

Nils thrust the king aside; the head rolled off. With one serpentine movement he was on his side, rubbing his hands down his hips, counterfeiting ecstasy. He finished the limerick in heavy, syrupy accents—

"Eet'z a vonderful theeng
To be onder a keeng,
Eez democracy better, I esk you?"

It was very slapstick and very funny. Cathleen clapped. They crowded around her to ask what she thought.

"I loved it. Nils is a born clown," she said. "But of course they won't let you put it on."

"Remember times are changing." Nils was sour with anticlimax. "It's not the forties, darling Mrs. Bell. Or even the fifties."

"Oh, they had sex in my day too," said Cathleen. "And I'm sorry, because it's funny and it's clever and you've worked so hard. But the headmaster will have to say thumbs down."

And he did.

11

They were all working hard now, with the examinations only months away. Rosamund was finishing the painting that was called her major work, but she whisked it off to school, where her art teacher could advise and criticise, so that Cathleen did not see the final version. Rosamund was whole-hearted about her art again, studying Rembrandt's drawings, Caravaggio's compositions, making quick sketches of a magpie's feather, of two boys at play, the ants' nest high in the Sydney peppermints. She took lessons in conversation from an old French lady with a hunched back and exquisite manners; she said that now she dreamed in French, a sign of complete familiarity with the language. She worked at the mathematics she detested, knowing this to be the price of entry to the faculty of her choice in the university of her choice. She and Sara (so gifted at the sciences, so logical and industrious and intelligent) had far outstripped the others and were running neck and neck for dux.

There was little time for fun, that last vacation. One barbecue, with Nils in the place of honour, switching roles from chef to maître d' as the mood took him. He was the only one with energy left to play the fool. As long as he got through (purely to satisfy the ancients, he was quick to explain) he did not care about the quality of his pass. So he talked to the sausages as he impaled them on a long fork, imploring them to be versatile or co-operative or even inscrutable—in fact any word he took into his head.

"Uneven hamburgers have great charisma," he pronounced, serving the jagged circles of meat. "A bonny little vintage," he whispered, as he poured out the lime-juice. His audience smiled, but was too fatigued to laugh at his clowning.

Cathleen surprised the group with her knowledge of Hamlet. She listened while they discussed Olivier's interpretation, Gielgud's, Burton's; then threw in some matter of her own.

"Hamlet couldn't have wanted to act," she said with authority. "That's one thing I'm certain of. Or when he caught the king alone—well, action was needed, not talk and excuses. And he didn't act did he? In the end we all do what we really want," she finished.

"How do you know about Hamlet, Mrs. Bell?" they asked.

"She can practically recite it by heart," said Rosamund, quite proudly. "She's a walking repository of all the plays."

"How come, Mrs. Bell?" they clamoured.

Cathleen felt a sudden pang of longing for her father, slumped in his chair at the window, or before the fire. How bored she had been. And now, how grateful! In all manner of situations Shakespeare's words had provided a running accompaniment of wit, or wisdom, of beauty, of sardonic comment.

"Oh, my father was a Shakespeare—buff," she said lightly.

They clapped her for the modish word. "Very well spoken," commended Nils. "Soon you'll graduate to the proper four letters. Come on, we'll start now. Which do you fancy? One that starts with sh or one that starts with f—,"

"Neither," said Cathleen. "They're both forbidden."

With the examinations only weeks away Cathleen besought Rosamund to put her painting aside and concentrate on swotting.

"Can't, mamma," said Rosamund. "If you did anything creative you'd know you've got to grab it when it comes. Keep in practice, but grab it by the tail."

"But you keep on ripping up what you've done. So—"

"But I'm learning, that's the thing. By the time I'm thirty I mightn't be too bad. Please don't fret, mum," she called after Cathleen. "I know as much as I need to know, I'll get my scholarship. Trust me."

So Cathleen trusted. At last they came, those sadistic tests; somehow, for good or for bad, they were tackled and done with. Rosamund was thin and cranky, but fairly pleased with her papers. At the school prize-giving she was dux, and Sara was given the outstanding student award, together with the two hundred dollars grant that went with it.

"How about swapping?" Rosamund pointed to the quite magnificent set of art encyclopaedias that had fallen to her lot. "I could use two hundred bucks."

In truth she was pleased for Sara, pleased for herself, pleased for all of her friends. Even before the official results they were

87

all sure that they had made the university of their choice. As for Nils, he said that he was entering the school of hard knocks, to study boot-licking and bum-crawling. In no time he had found himself an employer, a squat little Frenchman with olive skin and a superior palate; very knowledgeable, Nils said. Every year he took on a few novices to instruct.

"Like twenty froggies went to school," said Cathleen. "Maybe you'll end up like Master Bullfrog, teaching other little frogs."

"What's that?" Nils leaned forward, all agog. He wouldn't be satisfied until she had repeated the verses to him. He was charmed to hear that froggie was a synonym for Frenchman.

"A low-life synonym," Cathleen amended. "Well, I hope you have a happy apprenticeship. How long will you stay with him?"

"Not too long. In two years, I'll have sucked him dry and spat him out like a rotten pomme de terre." He spat graphically and blushed when the spit-ball landed on Cathleen's foot. "Sorry, Mrs. Bell." He took out a very white linen square and mopped it up. He looked at her and grinned. "Funny how quickly the year went."

"Oh Nils, they go faster and faster! I find they're absolutely galloping. By the time you get to my age—Yesterday's snowball is today's avalanche. It just isn't funny," Cathleen lamented. "As for tomorrow—"

"Tomorrow the deluge!" said Nils. "Après all of us the deluge. Who cares?"

The little girls who had smoothed hand-cream on their sunburned legs, and pulled the same brand of white socks over feet, hardened with six weeks of barefoot running—these little girls were a troop of damsels, their high school days only a memory; young women with sidelong glances, with graceful, colt-like movements and musical laughter (except sometimes when they forgot their lines, and burst into a cacaphony of raucous giggles). As for their clothes, they were as determined now to be different as they had once been determined to conform. Cathleen, cleaning the windows with methylated spirits and soft rags, looked down through the mulberry tree and listened to five of them, holding forth on the necessity to create their own life-style.

"Charisma, that's what we're aiming for," said Florence, and everyone nodded; charisma was the in word.

Very pompous, the young, thought Cathleen, stifling a giggle, watching a million baby spiders, just hatched, spindling down minute silken threads towards the ground. She had disturbed the egg-bag, and whoosh!

Patsy had arrived, bad news. The dogs barked at her. The girls smiled coolly. These days Patsy only came to skite.

She was skiting. "Don't know how I made it into Architecture. I didn't do a tap of work, not a single tap. That's what being in love does to you!" No one took the bait, so she tried again. "You can't imagine how divine it is to be in love."

"Who with?" Sara asked, at last.

"Peter, of course."

"You must be kidding;" they all scoffed.

"You've been knocking around with him since the ark," said Rosamund.

Even quiet Cass muttered, "You stay in love a long time, Patsy."

Patsy, insulted, decided that she'd leave. She stuck her nose in the air and flounced away. At the corner of the house she turned and yelled at them, "You're a lot of swine!"

"Good riddance!" said Liz, spitefully. "She only hangs on to that drongo because she doesn't have to sleep with him."

Liz, like all the others, had a constant turnover of escorts. From one season to another they were replaced, like so many accessories. It appeared that three months was the maximum time, the absolute outside that they could keep a boy on the bubble without bursting his boiler.

"If you understand what we're referring to, Mrs. Bell," said Florence, with some delicacy.

"Oh yes," Cathleen answered. "It came up in my day too. It might be termed a universal problem."

They discussed the pill, reasons for and against. Many of the young kids at school had been using it for years, silly little fools. Who but a zany would waste herself on those pimply characters? But later on—university men—poets, young doctors—men of the world—. Girls don't change much, Cathleen noted. They have a pretty good idea of their own worth, and they still want their first lover to be a passport to some better life; or a hero, as I did.

Rosamund had stopped bluffing about being a film director. She thought she would study Fine Arts, and French, Japanese perhaps, or Philosophy. It sounded interesting, but not very marketable, Cathleen thought, but did not dare to say.

Only one piece of advice did she offer. "Why don't you go to Tech., and really study your drawing? You could do with some donkey-work in technique. No?"

Rosamund shook her head. She had topped the State in Art; very satisfactory, she said. She had won second prize in a district art contest, for a surrealist picture of Nils as a dragon-fly, skimming over clouds like flowers reflected in a lake like a meadow. She had hashed it up in a couple of days, and was abashed and disconcerted with her prize. When people complimented her she hung her head, and muttered that it was crap. The prize-money she gave away at once, to a charity drive for war orphans. Nothing would persuade her to go to see her picture on display.

"Rosie, why not?" asked Sara. "It looks so striking."

"Oh Sara, it was a fake. I heard Murray was judging, and I know his work like the back of my hand. I just geared the thing to his taste. It was a disgusting thing to do. Venal! It was so shallow and impure."

Cathleen was puzzled. "I thought it caught Nils exactly."

Like a jack-in-the-box, Nils popped out of a buddleia bush. "That's because I *am* shallow and impure."

"How right you are!" Rosamund threw a crust at him. "Come and help me get the bread and honey for the lorikeets. Come to think of it, you're practically a lorikeet yourself. So gaudy, and you never stop chattering."

"Dragon-fly, lorikeet, which am I?" Nils loved to be the person centre-stage. "Can I have my picture, Rosie, when you get it back? It might be worth a million one day." He mused. "Then again, it might not."

"Do what you like with it Nils. I'm done with it. Keep it, burn it, rip it up, I don't care."

Nils was chewing a nasturtium leaf. "Why aren't you going to Tech., Rosie? You didn't tell us."

"I guess I'm frightened of being railroaded into doing things somebody else's way." Thoughtfully she licked honey from her fingers. Her nails, bitten to the quick during the examinations,

90

had grown again. "At school I was the best, so Johnno let me have my head and made such a fuss of me, all that jazz. But if I went to Tech. there'd be people more skilful than I am, and I might start wanting to copy them, I mightn't be able to help myself. And I'd lose my own vision."

"What is your vision, Rosie darling?" asked Nils.

"I'm not sure. It's something to do with despoiling the earth, and it's all tied up with myths and fairy-tales. And the terrible intricacies of our society, that's part of it too. The other day at Manning House, when I went in to enrol, I saw people all hugger-mugger after food, trays and trays of it, all different kinds. And on the window-sill there were two little birds, starlings, I think, picking up crumbs. It made me think. I tried to paint it, but it didn't go right."

"See!" Nils rolled over on his back. "In our decadent society food is supreme. If you can't earn a crust any other way, Rosie, you can come and paint murals in my eatery."

"Oh do shut up, Nils. You're always talking drivel."

"I'm off," said Sara. "When you two start sparring, it's time to get going." She went.

"Anyway, what I'm going to do is get myself a degree, so I can always be a librarian, or even a teacher—erk!—if I'm stuck for dough, which Heaven forbid," said Rosamund. "I'll work like a galley-slave. I'll be like Segovia, my own teacher and my own pupil. I'll paint out my fantasies as soon as I've got enough skill."

"Do you have fantasies too, Rosie?" asked Nils, popping his eyes and dropping his jaw to make himself look fey or effete or both. "Sometimes I see myself as Dracula. A terrible urge comes over me to sink my teeth into someone's luscious neck." In one lithe movement he was on his feet, he had Rosamund pinioned in his arms, and was nuzzling her neck. In another moment she had pulled free and swung to wallop him. Down they sprawled headlong on the grass, struggling pell-mell. Now one was on top, now the other. Now Rosamund had Nils imprisoned in a head-lock, moaning for mercy.

"You're a hefty wench," he grumbled, smoothing his hair. "A girl so muscly should be employed on the roads. Go and ask your Italian buddies to take you on."

It was an old joke with them, the immigrant Italian road-workers who whistled and wolf-howled after Rosamund. "Bella, bella," they called after her, that radiant fairness a sure hit with men used to darker beauties. Rosamund was very matter-of-fact about their paeans. She observed that the darker the guys, the better she went down with them; that a trip into town, round Paddington, say, brought forth a retinue of Turks and Indians and Lebanese.

She had an amused affection for the road-workers, the way they sprawled out after lunch under the robin-redbreast trees, legs akimbo like the farmhands in a Brueghel. She liked the handkerchiefs knotted over their heads, and their reeking makeshift dunnies, and their little huts with wooden benches outside, each one lined with tin dishes of clean water and square bits of hard yellow soap.

"They're like about seventy seven little dwarfs!" she had cried in delight, at the first sight of them. "Oh I do hope the roads take ages to widen!"

"No fear of that!" Cathleen answered drily. "They'd much rather give wolf-calls than work."

Now, years later, they were still on the job. They saluted Cathleen as an old friend when she passed with her shopping-basket. But for Rosamund, in the briefest of swimming costumes, a towel slung around her neck, they burst into a chorus of sighs and Latin applause.

"Who'd drive a car?" said Rosamund. "Think of the things you'd miss if you didn't go on foot. They'd have just been a scene, glimpsed for a moment out of a car window."

"Well, just don't swing those hips so lustiviously, Rosie," said Nils. "Or you might get more than you bargain for."

Cathleen was happy, that last holiday in the sun. The boys and girls who came to the house were filled with their new-found enthusiasms, so abrim with life that she felt herself honoured to be allowed to minister to them. By comparison, the teachers at her school, the matrons at the shops, all other quite-adults were frayed or jaded. All the causes they defended, these young ones, they defended with passion. They were so frank, so ardent, so dreadfully silly as they held forth on free love, compulsory sterilization, the ideal society.

Rosamund was beauty's champion. She dreamed of a fair world, where all bellies were filled, and nature triumphed over man's despoiling.

"But nature is cruel, Rosamund," Cathleen reminded her. "If man preys—why then he is no worse than the tiger—"

"Tigers have to be predators, that's their way. But men have brains. And they should have feeling hearts."

Sara and Liz were both getting cars, so that they could travel into university.

"You should be ashamed of yourselves," Rosamund scolded. "Adding to the pollution."

"But Rosie, they're only *little* ones." The girls wilted before the directness of her attack. "And we'll only use them when we have to."

"You'll see. You'll be dashing here and there like everyone else, tearing down to the shops when you need a—oh, a box of matches. Just don't talk about the rat-race, that's all. Because as far as I'm concerned you're both rats!" Rosamund's Irish eyes smiled at them, taking the sting out of her words. "Just you see, the petrol supply'll run out soon, and you'll have to cope without them."

"Oh Rosie, I'm getting a motor-bike!" cried Nils, teasing her. "Do you approve of motor-bikes?"

"God forbid!" said Rosamund. "You'll be a double amputee after your first ride, with a trail of dead bodies behind you."

Cass and David were holding hands. They thought they might get a flat together when David started at N.I.D.A. They swore Cathleen to secrecy; their parents were still on the old wavelength, white weddings and all that crap.

"When I look at the local rag and see all those brides who've been on the pill for years I could puke!" said Cass, quite fiercely. She looked as if she mightn't mind being one of the brides.

"Heavens above, it's all so different!" cried Cathleen. "The mothers get younger and younger. I saw a girl in a bikini with a fresh caesarean scar and a baby on her hip, wheeling a trolley around the supermarket. She couldn't have been more than fifteen."

"I saw a huge tall woman with a see-through blouse and e-normous nipples!" said Sara suddenly. "She was leading a

Great Dane with e-normous nipples too."

They all vied in telling what they had seen and heard and smelled and stored in memory. Rosamund had taught them that: it was her gift to them. "Use your eyes, use your senses, you only have one chance," she urged them, again and again. When she chose, she could charm the birds off the trees: she lived with conviction and with delight.

Liz, so static usually, was suddenly animated. "Rose, I saw your rabbit-ladies. I never really believed in them, but I saw them with my own eyes. They had cork on their eyebrows and mouths painted in ginger Cupid-bows." Everybody listened; they had all heard about the rabbit-ladies, who appeared in Alcheringa out of nowhere and scuttled back to nowhere. "They were all you said, exactly, rabbit fur sewn in tufts all over their capes—capes!—and little gold lamé bootees."

"Oh, lucky Liz!" mourned Nils. "I would give my—tongue,—even—or my palate—to see those dames."

Rosamund had the last word. "And I saw a kite-man rise suddenly over the cliff near Faggotter's," said Rosamund. "I was sitting there thinking, and the magpies flew up in a scare on to the angophora. I thought they were coming to get me, and I put my hands over my eyes."—

"The Frenchmen put their tin hats over their dicks," murmured Nils, "In the first war. That's a good four letter word Mrs. Bell for your collection. Also it is a well-known name," he added virtuously.

"Finished, Nils?" Rosamund hurried on. "Well I took my hands away from *my* most precious possession, and whoom, he came over the crest! All spreadeagled out, his limbs all whichways. He gave a terrible convulsive flap with his arms, and took off. The birds were gibbering. So was I."

"I expect they thought it was a giant predator bird," said Sara, gathering up the lunch debris.

"Oh, why can't they leave the skies alone!" Rosamund raged. "They've fouled up the roads and choked the sea with sewage and now they're hot-foot after the skies."

"Oh come off it Rosie. The heavens aren't going to suddenly spawn kite-men," said David.

"Who knows?" said Rosamund darkly. "It's all such a bloody mess!"

Cathleen was inclined to agree. She had always managed without a car, and was inclined to feel that much of the to-and-froing was excessive. Really, if you went overseas stupid, then you came back stupid, no matter how you tossed off the key names and the passwords. Harmless enough, she thought, unless you were poor Basil Levy— Still, it was disturbing to see Aldebaran metamorphosed into a tail-light.—

"See the herons!" called Rosamund. "Over there!" Her cheeks were red with excitement. The graceful birds stalked over the mangrove roots, looking for food. Billy pricked his ears, stretched, and caught sight of them. In a bound he leapt the fence. They lifted their heads, the herons; and they were gone. The air was chilled, the sun dropping.

"Summer is over," said Cathleen. "And my woodpeckers will fly back to Japan."

12

Seeing the young, so full of enthusiasm for this new step (not such a giant stride, really, not much more than an extension of school) made Cathleen conscious of her impoverishment of spirit. Each year she finished with one batch of children, and each year a new batch came to her. Each and every eternal year she disengaged them from their mothers, if they clung too tightly, or, if they were bumptious, administered the necessary squelch with smiling equilibrium. Once in a blue moon they gave her a change, but mostly not: she was stuck forever, it seemed, with kindergarten classes: having proved herself cut-out for the job, she had it for life. I am an old record playing the same tune over and over, she thought. Whatever variations she introduced, it was always the same theme. The span of each year was as inexorable as it was inevitable: summer term, split by Easter, then autumn, and projects on autumn; vacation; winter term split by book week; vacation, spring term; Santa Claus and Little Baby Jesus, followed by—thank God—vacation. Year after year after year. She could change the stories and poems, try to vary the handicrafts but the more she changed her programme, the more it was always the same.

One year she had the children bind picture-frames with raffia, and she photographed each child in turn, and stuck a photograph inside each scruffy raffia circle. The children were pleased with their own images, the mothers touched and charmed. One Christmas she made a plum pudding for the class, with each child contributing a portion of the ingredients and a few stirs with the wooden spoon. That was the year she said goodbye to the class she had taken on from kindergarten to first class, to second. She hoped that it would never happen again, it hurt too much to say goodbye. She had tears behind her eyes as she cut the pudding into slices, one for each child to eat, one to take home. Tears ran down her nose and over the plate heaped with neat slices; and that made them all laugh.

"Whoever gets the top slice gets salt in it," she said. Everybody wanted the top slice.

In all seasons, however, she tried her best. She took a great deal of trouble with the nature lessons, obeying Rosamund's behest that she must teach them to respect their environment.

"Teach them to stop tormenting," she ordered. "Stop them from pulling wings off flies and putting locusts in match-boxes. Tell them not to kill unless they have to, and then do the job quickly. And see if you can get them to stop littering the parks and the beaches. And listen, mum, tell them that legs are made to walk on. If you can teach them to respect all creation, they might learn to respect their own kind—Or even themselves," she added.

Quite often now Rosamund acted like a friend instead of an inquisitor. One morning she stood at the kitchen window, scrutinizing the bay, noting cloud-shape and bird-flight as she gulped her coffee. "I guess you set them a good example," she said.

"Do I?" Cathleen was pleased and surprised. "How?" she asked, eager for more of the same.

"Well mum, you aren't slack, are you? No sickies, and proper playground duty, and seeing to it that the skinny ones have extra milk, all that. And you don't play favourites, even when you want to."

"The trouble is," said Cathleen, in a voice watery with self-pity, "I come home all wrung out. Every day I'm squeezed as dry as that bit of old sponge you brought home from the beach. I've been thinking of what you said about developing myself, and I know you're right, but I'm just too tired"—

Rosamund had no time for self-pity. She changed the subject with some abruptness. "By the way, the cockroaches are in residence again. Last night I woke up, I could hear someone in my room, I was petrified. I didn't know whether I should scream or lie still or spring up and confront him. Then I realized that it was my old lute-guitar, plink, plonk, plink, plonk, someone was playing it up on top of that stack of junk in the corner. Very odd. I turned on the light and believe it or not it was a cockroach. A lute-playing cockroach."

Cathleen chuckled. "A lute playing the cockroach," she murmured.

Rosamund blinked at her. "Mum I said a cockroach playing the lute. Not the other way round." Very quickly, with a black chalk, she roughed out a demented lute strumming on a cockroach's belly; and shoved it across. "You're crazy, you say the maddest things."

"Sometimes I can't even think straight," said Cathleen. "Truly, sometimes I feel so woozy that my feet aren't touching the ground."

"Maybe you're menopausal," Rosamund suggested.

"I'm thirty seven," said Cathleen. "Not forty seven. No, I'll just have to shake myself out of my lethargy. I'll have to start going to the opera matinées. There's that beautiful opera house—"

"Oh, I think it's a botch!" cried Rosamund. The university had developed her natural propensity for criticism. Iconoclast by nature, she was surrounded and reinforced by iconoclasts. "The building's eye-catching, of course, but doesn't it look idiotic against a background of city. It should be surrounded by an immensity of space, sand, I think, or green lawns, so that it looks like an immense sea-monster come to rest in an immense garden. Can't you see that? Even if they'd put it round the next bend, well, it wouldn't be right, but it'd be better. Even you must see that!"

"Yes. Sort of," said Cathleen, meekly.

"But of course that's typical of our city, the absolute grossness of the things they're doing. Those filthy canyons!"

"Martin Place is nice." Cathleen knew that her defence was feeble, but she persisted. "The poplars are lovely, and the flower stalls, and the way they've closed it off. And the old post office with all those colonnades."

"But mum, can't you see it shouldn't be like that. One oasis! It should be all planned, all of it, an entity, not just hit and miss in the hands of the speculators and whatever architect they happen to get hold of. Can't you see?" Rosamund was all the more impassioned since she had taken up with an architecture student. "Laurence says he longs to tear it all down and start again."

"Mmm." Cathleen glanced at the clock, then allowed herself the luxury of another cup of coffee. "Still, some of the buildings are so old and decrepit, they'd have to be replaced, wouldn't they? And some of the new buildings are beautiful, don't you think?"

"It's the muddle!" shouted Rosamund. "What's the good of a few beautiful buildings in a junk-heap! It's old and new and gingerbread swags and concrete cubes all shoved together in one disgusting conglomeration. All the proportions wrong! As Laurence says—not that I listen to him, I've got my own eyes, so don't smirk, you silly old bitch!"

"Thank you," said Cathleen. "Flattery will get you nowhere, though."

"It's so seethingly, repulsively ugly. Oh if I could have a free hand, if only I had the doing of it, I'd gather a bunch of young architects with pure minds and—and aspirations, and I'd start from taws—"

"Laurence could head them," murmured Cathleen.

"Oh you're not too tired to needle me, are you?" In spite of herself, Rosamund gave a muffled snort of mirth. "Well, I've got my plans! If I were a Medici"—

"Well, you're not," said Cathleen. "You're only a Bell. So get going or you'll miss the bus and be late for lectures."

"Who cares?" Rosamund took off, still fuming. This was her year for championing causes.

It was strange. Rosamund had stopped jibing about her mother's passivity, but the seeds of discontent she had sown were sprouting. After all I am thirty seven, Cathleen mused, looking out over a windswept bay the colour and texture of dark grey flannel, rough as an old workman's shirt. Halfway through my life, probably. Am I to spend the next thirty years as a bystander? Two or three years and Rosamund will be gone. She has used my youth, eaten it up. Like the wasp that stings its victim, and leaves it immobile for its young to gorge on, I have stung myself, and left my own heart for her to munch.

Futile thought. No one forced me, I did it myself. And anyway I had myself to feed and clothe. She picked up her brief-case, hesitated, then put in a telescoped umbrella. It might rain. Be prepared, it always might rain. But next spring, or next year, she vowed, or whenever I stop being so tired, I'll start something new. I'll study philosophy, or play the harp, or join the National Trust, anything. But I'll have to do something to make a life for myself when Rosamund has flown the nest. She slammed the door, quite hard, bent to pat Billy and Bess, closed the gate on them. When she came home they would be at the gate, waiting for their victuals. How could days so empty be so full? "Walk me!" wagged the dogs. "Prune me!" cried the wisteria. "Paint me!" groaned the old walls.

No, no, they have no voices, said Cathleen, silently. The voices come from my own timidity and languor, my need to shelter behind tasks I impose upon myself.

"Coming to school with us, Mrs. Bell?" called the red-headed Walker twins. They were dragging broken branches along the dirt by the roadside.

Sooner or later they'd start whacking each other—or someone else—and they—or someone else—would come howling and bleeding to her, for sympathy. She unclenched their fists and prised the branches loose. A waste of time, really. They'd find new weapons as soon as her back was turned. Stop being so dreary, she admonished herself. And someday, somewhere, some gentleman of a certain age who has kept his figure and his aquiline profile— She quickened her steps, and the boys had to run to keep pace with her.

University: Rosamund and Sara, Florence and Liz, all of them, were seething with pleasure in their new freedom. Rosie is being courted by a Spaniard, they whispered. Laurence? Oh she got sick of him, he was just this side of a pansy, anyway—

Sara was prepared to spill the beans when Cathleen sounded her out.

"So handsome!" she murmured. "Of course he's only about two inches tall, very minuscule. He just about comes up to Rosie's ears. A curly black beard! He teaches Spanish in a Catholic girls' school."

"Imagine the havoc!" said Cathleen, lightly. "Is Rosamund smitten?"

"Not really. You know Rosie. Anyway, if she were really smitten I wouldn't tell you. As a matter of fact, I think she'd tell you herself if she were. She's much more fond of you than she ever discloses," said Sara.

"He lives on sunflower seeds and yoghurt. He meditates a lot," Florence confided. "I hope Rosie passes him on to me. We're more of a size."

With the coming of Rosamund, glare and all, they stopped

telling tales.

"I was asking the girls about Ramon," said Cathleen, to get them out of trouble. "They weren't telling on you."

Rosamund chose to be haughty. "How could they? There's nothing to tell. But just try minding your own business, will you, old woman?"

Cathleen tried, but she couldn't help wondering. It is past time for a lover for this girl all fire and ice and roses, who, surprisingly, happens to be my daughter. Vicarious living again. Sometimes Cathleen wondered whether it would be a man much older, to stand stead for the father Rosamund had never known. Still—young blood pulses hot, and youth's clarion calls to youth. Who made that up? Did I? My mind is a rag-bag of second-hand words. Everything at one remove, everything hand-me-down.

One afternoon, because she could not help herself, she tackled Sara.

"How old is he?" she asked the girl, who sat cleaning her toe-nails in the bay-window, pink toe-nails smooth as sea-washed shells. "You have very pretty toe-nails, Sara," she added.

Sara spent much of her time with Rosamund, now that her stepfather had come to rule her mother's house. Soon, she said, next year maybe, they would get a flat to share in town, she and Rosamund. She was unhappy at home since her father's death, and her mother's swift forlorn remarriage. As hasty as Gertrude's, Sara remarked, with dispassion, and to a man as swinish as Claudius. She began to paint her toe-nails, then looked up. "Sorry, Mrs. Bell. What did you say?"

"That—that Ramon." Cathleen felt rather silly saying his name. "But don't tell me if you don't want to."

Sara was evasive. "Oh, about thirty, or a bit more."

"Sara, do me a favour, will you? At that age he's been around, he knows all the ins and outs—"

Sara gave a guffaw. "Sorry," she breathed. "But that was a Freudian slip."

Cathleen didn't laugh. "She's so reticent, she'd tear strips off me for saying this. But Sara, you know Rosamund, she doesn't count the cost. Just see she's familiar with the pill, and how you've got to use it for a while to get used to it, all that—"

"But of course she knows all about it. I mean, it'd be pretty hard not to, don't you think? All the twelve year olds know. But you don't need to worry, Mrs. Bell. Rosie thinks he's terribly attractive, so carnal. Venal as well as incorporeal, you know. But she wouldn't get involved with him, he's too shallow." The cool fluty voice ceased; perhaps she had said too much. She bent the narrow perfect oval of her face over her narrow feet. She was silent.

What jargon they talked, these children. How could anyone be carnal and venal and incorporeal all at the same time! "I thought mysticism was his—his scene," said Cathleen.

"That's right, it is. That's what makes him so sex-crazed. He never stops talking all that stuff about body language. Hugh can't stand him. Of course Hugh's very down-to-earth," said Sara proudly.

Rosamund came up from the wood-shed whistling. "The sun's on the rim," she said. "Come on Sal, we'll brave it eh? Just one quick dip before dark."

"Don't go out far, girls. The life-savers won't be there."

Too late. They had gone. They were forever coming and going, scattering their lecture-notes, dropping their towels, boiling kettles. The old house rang with their laughter, the old boards creaked to their exits and entrances. And I am always staying, mused Cathleen, never going anywhere. Some day I will, though.

More and more now Rosamund was away from home. She was involved in a dozen different scenes, as they were called, each one with its own set of demands. In the short vacations she worked on essays; in the long vacation she followed the itinerant workers, hoping, as she put it, to make a fat wad for the year to come. Always, just as Cathleen thought that she couldn't bear the loneliness, Rosamund would turn up with a crowd of her friends, and it was on again: swimming, sailing, eating, talk, talk, talk.

Perversion and pornography were very big that summer. The cases for and against kinky sex were put forth again and again, demolished again and again. At the library Cathleen saw a book on homosexuality. Homosexuality for All: The New Creed, it was called. She longed to borrow it and fill out all the gaps in her understanding of the new creed, but she was too shy.

"Are there many of them at university? Gay—gay persons, I mean," she asked gamely.

Rosamund and Sara started to laugh. "A for effort, mum," said Rosamund. "You try very hard to keep abreast."

"Yes and no," Sara answered her. "There are little pockets of them, as I suppose there are in any intellectual milieu. Many a young fellow has been given a boost up because of his—um—delectable buttocks, I should imagine, the world being what it is."

"Oh!" Cathleen was dismayed.

"Actually they're rather attractive," Sara soothed her.

"It's the hypocrisy, not the homosexuality that I hate," Rosamund snorted. "Did I tell you, Sal, about Morgan le Fay translating some old French ballad? When he came to the bit about the whore's sexual apparatus, he called it the place of delight. Some hypocrite, eh? When you think what his notion of Cythera really is—"

"Place of delight," repeated Sara. "It sounds like a painting by Bosch."

Rosamund looked thoughtful. "Mmm," she said, turning up her palms and looking at them. Preoccupied, she stared out of the window.

As term-time came closer, Rosamund toyed with the idea of staying in town. Sara and Florence, Liz and a girl called Christina, and another called Joan had decided to rent a terrace house and pool expenses. One kitchen, one bathroom, every other room a bedroom. Rosamund thought that she would pay for a room (six dollars a week) and use it rather than catch the late bus home.

"That's a good idea," said Cathleen. "It's too much for you, coming home at one and going off again at seven. I'm glad."

"Who asked for your seal of approval? Surely at nineteen I can come and go as I please?" Cathleen turned away. This was going to be one of the difficult days. "And don't look so bloody martyred," Rosamund yelled after her.

103

"Why don't you stay in altogether?" Cathleen forced herself to say. "It's an awful lot of travelling. Just come home at weekends."

Rosamund was shamefaced. "Sorry, I didn't mean to yell. Yes, sometimes I will, as our work thickens up. But I don't want to leave you all alone."

"Just do what's best for yourself, darling," said Cathleen, with a heart as heavy as her voice was cheerful.

The question came up again and again, and was never properly resolved. Sometimes Cathleen came close to hoping Rosamund would go. For even now, how unpredictably and woundingly her temper blazed. How like her ruthless father she was as she stood all akimbo, granite-faced, with eyes of ultimate ice-blue. The years of adolescence had been hard enough, God knows, when the stubborn, self-willed (but loving, always loving) child was shedding her skin. But Cathleen had taken solace in the knowledge that the storms would pass, had understood the violence of the tides that surged within the young girl. And little by little, two steps forward, one step back, they had reached an armistice. Secrecy, then hostility, and then a blessed truce. Without much said it was understood that they trusted each other, that certain areas would be taboo, that certain values would never be shared. But on the whole they knew where they stood.

As Rosamund had said, speaking of Liz's practically nymphomaniac young sister, "Well, she's acting like a loon because she has to show her mother that she won't be pushed around. She's different from Liz. But she'll cool down. After all, she knows in the end that her mother's all for her. Even if it's just an extension of self—"

The conversation had begun amicably enough, then one word had lead to another and it ended in war. She knows I am for her, thought Cathleen. But is she for me? She turned blindly away from the girl who had just smacked her across the face. A bully. But if I hit her back, pick up anything and clout her, then who gets hurt most? Like all the wars: someone has to say calm down. She went into her room and sat on the bed.

Rosamund followed her. "It's incestuous, our relationship,"

she cried. For two or three days of the month she was a shrew. "Why don't you admit that you hate me?"

"Because I don't," said Cathleen, forcing tears back. "I deplore you."

"Well I admit freely and frankly that I hate the sight of you. Why won't you fight fair and square? Why didn't you hit me back?" Guilty and defiant she faced her mother.

"Because I'm not a pugilist," said Cathleen. "Because I don't believe in wars and I think it's immature to fight."

Rosamund's face softened for a moment before she was off again. "You're so hidebound. All those principles. Don't fight! Do your duty! Stay put! You're so boring!"

Cathleen's shoulders slumped. It was true, she had always been boring. At school, too boring to make more than a couple of friends. Too boring for Brian to take her with him. A brown wren, an echo. And now, ultimately, my child finds me a bore.

"You're so right," she said in a low voice.

"Oh, you are a wicked woman! That's your specialty, making people feel guilty. That's how you keep me chained!"

How could she share a life with someone so full of hate? "Go then! Go wherever you like!" Cathleen cried. "Live in town or throw up your course, do what you like. Quit! Go bare-legged round the world with a knapsack on your back. But remember you won't be young forever, and you'll be glad some day to have a job to come back to."

"What for? So I can skulk in a hidey-hole like you? You've been nowhere. What do you know about anything but this backwater? You've never seen the sun come up over the Aegean, or felt the winds sweep in across the Aran islands—Or—"

"You sound like a travel pamphlet," said Cathleen coldly, for once giving as good as she got. "No, I haven't, and I probably never will. It's my nature to put down roots."

"Well it's not mine!" shouted Rosamund. "And when I've finished this bloody course I can tell you I'll be off."

Cathleen was relieved to hear that she intended finishing. Stupid not to, when she had almost reached halfway. By now she knew better than to make a noise of approbation. What she really needs, Cathleen thought again, is a lover. She looked at the girl before her, luscious and ripe as summer fruit, stormy as clouds massing for a summer downpour. Really, she thought, I never sank serpent's teeth into my parents' hide—but times were different then, I was a child and protected, and nobody told us then that we hated our parents' guts.

"I'm going in to the dump to stay for good," called Rosamund from her room. "Or at least for the rest of the year. It'll do us both good." Tall and fair in the multistriped dress that Cathleen had ironed for her that morning, with a duffle bag over her shoulder, she came to say goodbye. "Well, if I hurt you I'm sorry. You'll have quite a bruise there!"

"You're a bully!" said Cathleen. "I don't like bullies." For once she didn't offer to retract. "I love you very much, Rosamund, but I hate that cruel streak in you."

"Well, that's the way I am," said her daughter, stooping to pat Bess and Billy. "Bye, dogs. There's something about you that gets me, though. You ask to be hurt." And she was gone.

For the rest of the year she stayed in town. From time to time she telephoned, from time to time she came home for a few hours. But when she came she was only perching.

"You've got to learn to do without me, mum," she said on one visit—for her air was that, of a visitor only. And I've got to learn to stop using you as a buffer."

"I know. We'll both learn," said Cathleen.

She was lonely that year, it was true, but mostly she was tired. She no sooner got rid of one cold than she caught another. She felt so depleted that she hardly had the energy to miss Rosamund; in fact she was glad that she no longer had to cook meals for the horde of starving young who had picked her cupboards bare. She pushed herself along to her job: she despised slackness and loafing. Sometimes she thought she should go to a doctor, but there was nothing specific she had to tell him. So she bought a tonic from the chemist; and as spring came she felt a little more ready to begin each day.

She waited Rosamund's pleasure: it had been her decision to go, and it was for her to make what moves she willed. And on her twentieth birthday Rosamund telephoned. Her voice sounded strained.

"Is anything wrong?" Cathleen asked, in sudden fear.

"Yes. No. Nothing that can be helped. I'm quite well, if that's what you mean. Nothing for you to worry about."

"Truly?" Cathleen asked.

"Yes, truly. Mum? Are you still there? I'll tell you about it at Christmas. All I rang for, really, is to hear you say many happy returns of the day. And to ask if I can come home for the long vacation. Or part of it, anyway."

"Please do," answered Cathleen, managing to conceal her jubilation. "Goodbye, darling. Take care of yourself."

13

And now, in the blinking of an eye, it seemed, the friends who had flocked were dispersed. Asked what had happened, Rosamund shrugged. Gone with the wind, she said, blown this way and that, paired off some of them, or abroad, or outgrown. Everything changes, nothing stands still, she reminded her mother.

So true, thought Cathleen. Soon I shall have no role left. My grandchildren's grandmother, maybe. She looked at the orange that Rosamund was kneading in her hands, preparing to stick it with cloves, and pack it away in some dark closet, where it would shrivel. Like me, she thought. No future for either of us.

Rosamund was deeply restive. She had freed herself of entanglements, she said, so that she could breathe again. Sometimes she stood moodily at the window, watching the summer showers. It never seemed to stop raining that summer. The hot sun steamed the water in the puddles, sucked it into the heavens; and at night it came down in torrents, drumming crazy music on the tin roof.

At twenty Rosamund was long-limbed and robust, clear-eyed, tawny-haired, not pretty but, her mother thought, probably beautiful. The blue arrows of her gaze pierced and disconcerted: no pretence or duplicity could escape their sting. She went to work, without pay, at an orphanage for spastic children, and came home each night to throw herself on the bed in a fit of hot tears.

"I don't think I can stick it there. Poor little buggers, they should be given a whiff of something lethal at birth. No one to love them, such terrible handicaps. Oh it's wicked!" She quieted her sad heart a little by adopting four Asian waifs: long distance charity, she declared, I'm too much of a coward to work at close range.

She painted furiously, fiercely, like one goaded from within. When Cathleen asked to see her work, she leaped in front of the big sheet of masonite.

"Wait till I've finished. When I've done it, then you can see, anyone can see it then. But I've got to get my childhood dreams and terrors down before they go beyond recall. I can feel them receding now—in a minute they'll be gone forever."

Cathleen remonstrated. "You'll go crazy, staying inside painting hour after hour, day in, day out."

"Leave me be, mum," said Rosamund. "Soon I'll be all painted out, and I'll have nothing to say till I do some more living. But I've got to keep on till it's done. Don't fuss. Next week I'll call up Sara and Liz and get myself a job or a bloke or something. But just leave me alone now. Please."

"You seem so disturbed," said Cathleen. "I can't help worrying. Something must have happened in that terrace house this term, to make you so shaken. You seem so different."

Rosamund, kneeling over the painting on the floor before her, refusing to use an easel, unorthodox in this as in all things,—Rosamund looked up.

"Christina killed herself," she said flatly. "She was working too hard, and she had a fight with her boy-friend. She was very undernourished, skin and bone, you couldn't get her to eat anything. She took poison. It was awful!" Her face was very drawn, very taut, almost hard in its impassive acceptance. "They took her to hospital, but she died anyway, on her twentieth birthday. Our birthdays were on the same day. It shook us all up, I can tell you. We all blamed ourselves for not doing something to stop her—though who could have guessed—"

"How ghastly!" Cathleen contemplated the girl's neck, strong but slender, bent over a kaleidoscope of colour. "Were her parents distraught?"

"What d'you reckon? Their only child!"

Too terrible to dwell on. Cathleen took a deep breath. "And her boy-friend?"

"Oh, he's got himself another bird. Men don't care much, I reckon, young ones at least. She was just someone to go to bed with. Actually, that was what made her take the poison. They had a row, and he said some pretty terrible things to her. He told her she was just his spare eff. Like a spare tyre. Nice, huh. See, she wasn't a sleeping-around type at all, she really cared about him. So when he let fly, she felt she didn't much want to go on living. I guess she felt—"

"Degraded," said Cathleen, almost to herself, remembering the raw pain of betrayal.

Rosamund's glance was speculative, her voice rather hollow. "Yes. In fact, that was the word she used. She stayed up all one night talking to me, and I thought she was over the worst. But two days after—kaput! Actually," she said slowly, "I blame myself a bit. Because it was the week before her period, and she was always terribly low then. I don't suppose she was eating much, she always just picked at her food—I was trying to swot for an exam, so after the first night I didn't go out of my way to dry her eyes. Really, I thought she had to get over it herself. I'd helped her through the first bit—Oh damn!" said Rosamund, miserably. "It was such a waste. It made us all take a good look at ourselves. I swore I'd try never to do anything shabby again. That's why I got rid of Paul—oh you didn't know about Paul did you?—I was only using him because he was a *catch*. And I also thought I wouldn't try for the university medal, because I didn't believe in that, either. Pot-hunting, I mean."

"What do you believe in, then?"

The clear brow knitted. "Loving-kindness, I think. And nature all-powerful. And in working hard at what you believe in—hence my furious activity here." She pointed to the stack of finished canvases. "And boring things like doing your duty— things like mothers who do their best for their ungrateful young." Obliquely said, it nevertheless was something that Rosamund had wanted to say. She was smiling, the singularly sweet and bounteous smile that no one could resist. "Look at my picture if you like," she said, and stood aside.

If I die this moment, I'll think it was worth it, thought Cathleen. If she punches me in the belly (as once she did) or bites me on the leg (as once she did) I'll still be glad—She looked down at the jungle of griffins and unicorns and dragons, all watched over by a malevolent old witch, one-eyed and evil. Why, Cathleen discovered, it's a travesty of Mrs. Llewellyn, a hundred times uglier, why, did Rosamund really see her like that? No wonder she shuddered away. In the corner of the picture slept two beautiful girls, one golden haired, one swart as a gypsy. Ignorant of the sleepers, cut off by a tanglewood of mythical beasts and boskage like serpents, ready to plunge into the tanglewood, stood—stretched really, so tall and languid that his head cleaved the clouds—a prince of the first water, with high Slav cheekbones and pointed ears. From his sword dripped, not blood, but rose-petals; and on the rose-petal cheeks of the blonde child were tears of blood.

Rosamund stood quietly until Cathleen had looked her fill. "Well?"

"As you know, I'm totally ignorant of composition and tone values, all of that. So I can't say anything about technique," Cathleen said, picking her way among a throng of impressions. "But—well, it is very strange and mystical. It tells me that if I had the key I could unlock the door into Eden. But I think that the key will never be found."

Rosamund was smiling to herself. "The pangs that guard the gates of joy," she murmured. "That was very perceptive of you, mamma. And as a reward," she added lightly, but with the telltale quiver in her voice that Cathleen had heard again and again over twenty years, "since you have earned it, I'll show you the other one I'm satisfied with. Or at least not dissatisfied."

She went into her room and came out with an oblong of hardboard, propped it up on the table, and stood back, waiting.

Cathleen caught her breath with pleasure. It was a painting of two young lovers, romantic yet somehow mondaine. Their feet spurned the ground. The insignia of sex were transmuted to flowers, the girl's breasts were as gauzy as the bubbles that floated away from her questing hands. A peacock spread his jewelled tail to make their carpet; a rainbow spanned the melting blue of sky, then dissolved into a shower of dew. The faces of the lovers were untouched and exquisite: alone, untroubled they walked in Eden. Colour and form, they seemed to vanish as she gazed: illusion. All that was left was iridescence.

"All loving mere folly," said Cathleen at last. "You think it's going to be like that?"

Rosamund nodded, "And is it?"

"For a while, if you're lucky."

"I expect I won't be," said Rosamund. "Now that I'm twenty, I'm starting to get a bit sceptical. So I thought I'd better paint it out, before I quite stopped hoping and believing."

"There's nothing to say that you can't feel like that at any age."

"I should think it's an essentially childish expectation," said Rosamund, with firmness. "And anyway, since novelty is of the essence, it's bound to dissolve. In the end I suppose I'll settle for a compromise job, like everyone else in the world, or nearly. Just as long as we're going the same way.—"

"I think you might well be happy with an older man. One who's learned his strengths. You find the boys so immature."

"Maybe." Rosamund cut her short. She had said all she wanted to say, heard all she wanted to hear. "I'm going for a walk. Some place where there aren't any cars. Because next to cruelty and wars and senseless destruction I hate noise and perpetual motion." She whooshed her pictures and herself out of sight. From the recesses of her room she called to Cathleen. "I might go and see Sara's grandmother. I promised Sara I'd look in from time to time. She's in that old convalescent home in Cabbage Tree."

Rosamund came back from the walk glowing. In the ten miles she had tramped she had feasted, found rich fare for eyes and ears and nose; she had renewed herself. She had the magical gift of taking beauty into herself, and giving it back again to all who touched her. The odd passionate child was a singular passionate young woman. Today everything in her world was beautiful. The turpentine trees were dripping with blossoms and nectar, so laden that the bees could scarcely stagger away with their hoard of sweets. How absurd they looked with their striped bums stuck out of the cream blossoms! And the air in the gully was so heavy with honey that you reeled, she said—oh those turpentines, so moth-eaten usually, they were practically *bridal*. And the acres where they grow the crops for the zoo, no words could describe their vibrant green, no paint either. And three ravens—or crows—they were like the ravens in the old ballad, they sat on a casuarina as still as skeletons, then up and away! they whirred off, wings glinting blue-black as the sunlight hit them.

She was a cauldron of bubbling words. Fennel, giant fennel, feathery though, and great big sunflowers as big as sliced pumpkins, and as orange. And in a ragged garden overgrown with morning glories, that pale one, a very tender blue—in the middle of the morning glory jungle stood a little ragged boy nursing a duck.

"Wait," she said. "You ain't heard nothin' yet." She had not even begun to praise old Mrs. Simpson, rising a hundred, deaf and frail and invincibly happy, reading her Bible, pronouncing

112

it very good literature, recommending it. Looking out from her window at the pageant of life along the road to the beach.

"Mamma, she has to be seen to be believed! She's so rickety she's hardly alive, but she's in the thick of life. A hundred nearly! She says she's like the Lady of Shallott, looking out of her window, she says it's unlikely that she'll ever spot Sir Lancelot. She's got a laugh like a rusty old kettle, and she's nearly stone deaf, but she knits rugs for the Salvation Army and she's so bloody happy that its beaut to be anywhere near her!" cried Rosamund. "No don't go, I've got more to tell you."

"I called in to see that little man in the nursery that's one hell of a tangle, but he knows where everything is and he loves his plants. He doesn't try to cheat because he doesn't believe in cheating. And all the way back there were dozens of kookaburras tuning up. And, listen, I saw a koala jump from one tree to another, simply miles—well, yards anyway. I held my breath." She looked down at Billy panting at her feet. "But it was too far for little Billy. He was alright going, but coming back was too hard."

Cathleen felt a stab. She looked down at Billy, panting, quite done in. Nothing lasts forever. Rosamund was raiding the refrigerator, starving, ready to eat anything that met her eyes. She looked filthy, like a goose-girl in a fairy-tale.

"Rosamund. Don't you think you should be seeing some of your friends? Those nice boys. Where's Nils?"

With her mouth full Rosamund answered. "Didn't I tell you? He won some very prestigious (as he put it) award for wine-tasting, or the like. He's off in France, treading the grapes. He won't be back till next year, if then. Why? Would you like him back for another little flirtation?"

Cathleen shook her head. "I'm not up to it. I couldn't even wink back at him. No, I just don't like to see you so solitary."

"Sometimes I need to be alone. I'm just resting between engagements, mum. Tomorrow I'll start pulling the old fence down, it's had it. One more storm'd do it in. Is there some good old guy who'll give me a hand? I can't get the hang of sawing fast—and I really need someone with a post-hole digger."

"But surely one of your university friends?"

"No, mum. If they came, which they wouldn't, they'd try to screw me instead of the fence. Truly, don't look so aghast.

That's the newest way to use up your body."

"An old one, it seems to me." Cathleen racked her brains.
"But, I think you're right, there should be a strong old man on a
pension. Look, I do know one, old Mr. McKenzie, along from
the school."

Rosamund, never one to let the grass grow under her feet,
went up the road in the early morning, and came back with a
willing helper. Mr. McKenzie, sturdy Scot, was part of the
landscape of Alcheringa. He did odd jobs around the school,
free, because, as he said, somebody had to do them. He minded
the dogs that had followed the children to school, and kept
them safe till home-time. He patched up guttering and painted
the high gables for old widows, who clung on to the old houses
where they'd brought up their children, and obstinately refused
to be relegated to a spic and span unit.

He followed Rosamund up the garden path, four steps back,
his eyes never leaving the cleft melon that was her behind, tight-
clasped in green pants.

The old lecher, thought Cathleen, half-amused, half-revolted.
He must be seventy. Or eighty.

When she told Rosamund, she was roundly admonished for
the possession of a dirty mind. "Just a decent old workman,"
she scolded. "And half-blind as well. He was probably just
peering out his way—Anyway he's going to help, very cheap
labour, almost sweated really, when you think what the new
breed charges. He's going to order the timber tonight. He says
he was a master builder in Scotland."

"And was he?"

"Maybe, maybe not. Who cares? He knows enough about it
to build your fence. And he does own a post-hole digger."

He did not ask exorbitant wages, the master builder: his
demands were of another order. Tentatively, at first, then
openly, he began to pay court to Rosamund. By the time the
holes were dug and the posts set in place he was in full cry after
her.

One day, one memorable day, when a sudden storm blew up
from the west, he came inside and sat for a long hour while he
told them the story of his life. Of his war years, of his wife and
children bombed before his eyes: a terrible story. Was it true?
Surely no one could make up such a tale? He burst into tears as

114

he finished. Rosamund had no doubts. She flew across the room and flung her arms about him. Blazingly honest, she could never believe that a tale as harrowing could be fabrication. But Cathleen saw a glint of something like triumph in his face when he took off his glasses and dried his eyes.

"How terrible," Rosamund was almost crooning over him, almost loving him for the sadness of his story, a latter-day Desdemona. She turned to her mother a face crumpled with pity. "Oh, life is sad," she keened and took his roughened hands in hers.

Damn, oh damn, thought Cathleen. I hope this fence is done pretty soon. The silly old goat! Pity and amusement were mixed with her vexation.

Each day now he grew more gallant and more lewd. He made salacious jokes about Billy who had held up all traffic before the newsagent's while he made a play for a blue cattle bitch almost, not quite, on heat.

Rosamund had stopped being sorry for him. "Get him off my back, mum." she said with desperation. "He's like a satyr. With that pipe of his—"

"Phallic symbol? Don't say you weren't warned—"

"Funny!" Rosamund groaned. "As soon as he starts whistling through his teeth I know he's going to harangue me about the erotic practices of Greek shipowners—Sprunting, he calls it."

"What?"

"Truly. How they take girls out on their yachts in mid ocean—and wham! And he's dyeing his hair—"

"The old buzzard!" cried Cathleen. "And I thought he was so nice."

"He *is* nice. Kind and strong and hardworking. Mum," she said weakly, "he's going to ask me to marry him. He keeps hinting."

"But Rosamund—" Cathleen was bewildered. How could he, that decent (or indecent) old workman, aspire to a girl fifty years younger. Flirtatious glances—heavy gallantries (rather charming, they sounded in his Scottish voice)—even off-colour jokes—well, they were one thing. But marriage—

"You're imagining it."

"No way. I play dumb, but while we hammer on the palings he tells me about the money he's got put by, how he needs a wife to brighten up his home, he keeps asking would I like a trip overseas."

"Oh they all ask that," Cathleen started to laugh, and found herself unable to stop. "But it serves you right, Rosamund, for telling him that the old men were steadier and had more stuffing than the young ones."

"Yeah! I guess that was the word that set him off." Rosamund was laughing too, choking with laughter. "Oh Lord, don't they ever get too old? Anyway the fence'll be done tomorrow. Lord, what a mess. I don't want to hurt his feelings, he's a nice old guy, those two little cats of his were dumped at the school, you know— How about taking him off my hands mum?"

"What?" Cathleen was affronted. "He's thirty years older than I am. More!"

"Well, anyway, when he comes to declare himself, say I'm too young and silly. Or riddled with pox. Or taking up a travelling scholarship, anything you like. Just get rid of him. I'm going in to stay with Sara and Hugh till he gets lost."

"You coward!" said Cathleen. "But maybe you're imagining it. Please don't go, I won't know how to say it."

"Yes you will." Rosamund had her duffle bag by the handle, and was shoving clothes in at full tilt. "Where's my clean pants? Oh, there! As you often remind me, I'm socially inept." She came out of her room and gave Cathleen a light kiss on the hair. "You cope, huh?"

Against her will, Cathleen coped. When she saw the square figure, so jaunty, so rejuvenated, swinging through the garden she wanted to run. Instead she opened the door.

"Where's Rosie?" he greeted her, without preamble.

"Oh here you are, Mr. McKenzie," cried Cathleen in a bright tinny voice. "Rosie? Oh, she's gone to stay with friends."

"When's she coming back?" He stood fair and square before the door.

"She didn't say," faltered Cathleen.

"She's run away, my little bird. Ah she's a wild one. Like your Billy," he added, with an unutterably silly smirk on his face.

"She'll finish the fence by herself when she comes back. So please may I pay you, Mr. McKenzie. Not that I can ever repay your kindness," said Cathleen, quite wildly.

"I'll wait for her to come and work along with me, my little mate." He gave a smile of the purest tenderness which nevertheless showed all his ancient teeth.

Cathleen almost stamped for anger, almost wept for pity. That fiend of a girl, to leave her this job. She sat down on the verandah swing, and motioned him to her side. "Please sit down. I have something to say to you."

He got in first. "I'll take care of your bonny wee bairn," he promised. "I won't let the wind blow on her. Anyone that touches her's got me to answer to."

Cathleen put her hand on his knee. "Please," she said, disgusted to hear her voice pitched between a bleat and a whimper. "I guess you're saying that you care for Rosamund—"

"Care! I'd give my life for her." Decent and idiotic, he glared at her with eyes of faded blue behind thick glasses.

"Rosamund never had a father," said Rosamund's mother. Much less a grandfather, she added to herself. "So I am very grateful for your kindness to her. And so is she." The prissy words hung in the air between them.

"Mrs. Bell, I'm asking to marry your girl!" he exploded. "I'm not young, it's true, but I'm not one of your fly-by-nights. I've got a bit of money put by and a house to take her to. The day I carry her over the threshold, that'll be the proudest day of my life."

Love had driven him out of his wits. Distracted. Or sunstruck on the long hot days.

"I'm sure you've misunderstood her feelings for you."

He shook his head. "No chance," he said, as firmly rooted in his madness as Malvolio. "She told me right at the start she had no time for the young flibertigibbets. The old ways and the tried and true, that's what she likes. She's shy as a bird, that's why she's kept it from you."

The stubble on his chin was grey. His nose was starting to splodge, an old man's bottle nose. "Stop it!" cried Cathleen, desperately. "She's not going to marry you or anyone. She's run away as she always does when the question comes up." She could not bear his wounded gaze, the fishlike opening and shutting of his mouth. "She asked me to tell you that she is much honoured by your regard." Oh you beast Rosamund, she said silently, into the silence.

"She doesn't want me then," he said heavily, getting to his feet.

"She does—doesn't want anyone," stammered Cathleen, and launched into a glib speech. "As you said, she's a wild bird, she can't bear to be caged."

His shoulders sagged, and he whistled soundlessly through his teeth. "I'd best go and finish the fence, then," he said, not without dignity. He picked up his pipe.

All morning Cathleen heard him working. Her nerves were on edge by noon, when he came to say goodbye. He took the money she gave him—twice as much as he had asked—without argument and without zest. Her heart was heavy for him. "Thank you for all your good work," she said. "Mr. McKenzie, thank you."

He gave the ghost of a smile. "It won't fall down in a hurry," he told her. "Well, if your girl needs me she knows where to find me." Square and solid, lustful but not jerry-built, he made off down the path. Cathleen wanted to wring Rosamund's neck. A mother gets saddled with some despicable jobs, she reflected. Who, given the choice, knowing beforehand what lay in front, would elect to be a mother? She gave a little shrug, and went back into the house. All of us, I suppose, she thought ruefully, poor mugs that we are.

14

When Rosamund came home a week later, the coast was clear. The weather, after a week of patchy rain, broke fine; one cloudless day followed another.

"Thanks mum." That was all the payment Cathleen got for the vile morning's work which her ungrateful child had foisted on her. She had two people in tow, Sara and a young Fine Arts student, very dirty, with a measly beard and a plummy voice. He was so anxious to please that he was almost non-existent. He stayed for three days, out on the verandah in a sleeping bag, or in his panel-van, discussing Caravaggio and begging Rosamund to go to Woolgoolga with him.

"Listen, bo, if you mention Caravaggio again, I'll castrate you," said Rosamund finally. "He's just about my favourite painter, and you're making me hate his guts."

Insulted, he took off.

"Good riddance," said Rosamund, "I thought if I insulted him enough he'd get the message. Did you notice how he stank? Imagine being cooped up in a van with him with the windows closed. It'd be like the Black Hole of Calcutta."

"Perhaps that's how he makes his impact," suggested Sara. "Why would you have the windows closed, though?" When Rosamund rolled her eyes and panted lustfully, Sara gave her pretty infectious giggle. "Sorry. Dumb, aren't I."

Sara had a few days to spend in Alcheringa, because Hugh had gone back to Cobar to see his parents. She was wholly committed to him; they had been living together for some months, and she was blooming. As Rosamund said, it was almost enough to make you believe in love. She liked Hugh, he was nearly good enough for Sara. There was no vestige of the old school rivalry between the two girls: they shared a loving friendship. No two sisters could have been more loyal or lovingly concerned for the other's good. Liking and admiring Sara for herself, Cathleen loved her for her affection for Rosamund.

They took Cathleen with them in the early mornings when they raced all-comers to be the first to make footprints on the wet sand after the night's high tide. Seagulls squawked and scattered as Billy and Bess ran headlong towards them. Pale green, still unpolluted—for how long?—the long beach awaited them. The king tides, the Christmas tides, had washed the sand away, changed the shape of the beach, tumbled rocks into a haphazard pile, playblocks discarded by a giant's child grown tired. Most of the sand had been dragged away from the roots of the Norfolk Island pines, fifty feet high or more; the knotted roots lay exposed.

"Look, Sara," Rosamund stared with fascination at the roots that reached out and down for support and sustenance. "They're dead but they won't give in."

"I daresay they're trying to hold on grimly until the tides bring the sand back again."

"Will it?" Rosamund looked to Sara for reassurance.

Sane and optimistic as always, Sara nodded. "I should think so. Look, they're firmly anchored on the side away from the sea. It's just a matter of holding on."

It always is, thought Cathleen. "I saved a child's life here, or near here, ages ago," she remembered aloud. "And because of that one thing all my own life was different."

"I remember. I think I do. I was standing by the water's edge and a huge wave broke over me. And you shouted at me to go back. You pulled me up the beach, you dived in—"

"You're a heroine," said Sara lightly.

"Is she ever!" said Rosamund, with equal lightness.

They turned and ran into the sea, both of them, dived into a wave together, and came up spitting and spluttering. Cathleen sat down to watch: she didn't feel like swimming today. How happy I am, she thought, to live at last in a climate of love, as I did when I was a child. In the end it was just a matter of hanging on: the bad years seemed far away.

Before the first wave of surfers came they were walking homewards, through the just-waking township. The first motorists were starting the long drive into town: soon the salty air, now tangy with sea-weed and eucalyptus, would stink of petrol. A young mother was hanging napkins on a clothes line; near her, in a play-pen on the grass, a baby was rattling the bars and screaming.

"Golly, listen to that," Sara marvelled. "I don't think I want a baby."

"If it's yours it's different. Still horrible, but you can't run out on it. Toddlers are unspeakable. But adolescents are worse."

"The same reason, I suppose," said Sara, thinking it out. "Trying to find their way in a new country."

"No wonder the parents run out. Mum nearly ran out." Cathleen shook her head. "You can't though. Even if it's a ghastly mess, it's a mess of your own making."

"So you blame the parents for the kids taking drugs, etcetera?" Sara, neat as a bird, had her head on one side.

"Who else? Please Sara, do we have to talk about the drug problem and overpopulation. Can't we just *be*?"

But Rosamund wasn't listening to them; the music that she heard was the old pods, last year's crop clicking like castanets on the jacaranda. "Sorry," she said. "Did I miss something? Look, Sara, they've lost their lustre, those shells we gathered. Only five minutes ago—" She opened one hand to show them.

Outside the paper-shop they bumped into two boys and a girl, old acquaintances it seemed. They had just bought the newspapers to look for their results. Rosamund and Sara had not bothered: they thought it lacked flair to hustle around after results. It never occurred to them that they might not pass.

"We all got through," said the girl, Judy Someone. "In everything. Sara, you were second in Chemistry. Rosie, you were second in French, and pretty high in Fine Arts."

"Good on us," said Rosamund. "See mamma, I told you we'd make it."

The two boys, sometime students, were gloomy; they had failed. They were half ashamed, half elated. They thought they might tour Australia and pick up any work they could for a year or two.

"What's that in your hand, Rosie?" one of them asked. The tall dark boy wrenched her hand open, quite brutally, to disclose a squashed orange toadstool.

"Same old Rosie," he said.

"You turd!" said Rosamund, with fury, and made off at top speed. When they caught her up she was still angry. "I wanted to paint that toadstool. I'm so glad he failed, that bastard. Serves him right for what he's done."

"For crushing your toadstool?" Cathleen was incredulous.

"For being one of the destroyers. He always was, wasn't he Sara? Punching up the little kids, lying and cheating—"

"He seemed a nice enough boy," Cathleen was bewildered by the hardness and anger on the two young faces. "I was wondering why you didn't ask him home."

"Tell my innocent mother. She'll believe you, Sara."

"He's the dregs," said Sara. "He's a drug pusher."

"He doesn't even take them himself—" Rosamund trembled with the force of her hatred. "If I could just have one wish, I'd have him blow up. He's a viper!"

"Calm down Rosie," said Sara. "One of these days one of his victims'll do the job for you."

By February it was over, that halcyon time. The two girls had gone somewhere on a train, cherry picking. School had begun.

Cathleen sighed, and made ready. It was curious, in the holidays she felt quite well, not vervy, but well, and after a few weeks in the hurly-burly of teaching (not such a hurly-burly, really) she felt like a rag. Maybe I don't really like my job, it's psychosomatic; because as soon as I slow down I feel better. Be quiet, she admonished herself: count your blessings, get started on your programme, and stop wallowing—So she did.

Rosamund's term started later, in March. She had not decided yet whether to share a house with a group of Fine Arts students. The sad impact of Christina's death had not been dispelled by the vacation. It was her last year at university; then she would be gone. She shilly-shallied between the duty she felt to spend this last year with Cathleen, and her natural inclination to live on the job where things were happening. And travelling took so long. In the end she decided to go, but to come home for weekends.

She was excited about going back. In Fine Arts they had a new lecturer.

Cathleen listened while she did the ironing. Whenever Rosamund came in she was accompanied by a mass of dirty laundry—She said that the facilities in Rose Street were non-existent, two old tubs and a broken copper. Also the air was so smutty from the factories that everything got filthy on the line.

"So that's why you're lucky, ma," she said, up-ending the bag at Cathleen's feet. "Also—you're an expert."

"Mmm." Now the expert laundress had almost finished demonstrating her expertise. But she demanded a price: that she be entertained while she toiled.

"Go on," said Cathleen. "Tell me more."

In a narrative punctuated by mock-sighs Rosamund told more. "He's so skinny you could snap him in two. So handsome—we all swooned at his feet."

"Is he married?"

"Many times over, I should think. Both in church and out of it. He looked us all over with an expert's eye. Did I tell you Florence failed? They won't let her in again. Not that she cares."

For a week or two, when she came home, Rosamund was full of the wonders of the new lecturer. A doctor of philosophy. A painter. A poet.

"All three? How can you be all three?"

"He does the most evocative sketches, very spare, rather in the Japanese manner, reeds or irises or lilies—he's very strong on lilies—or a seagull in flight, that sort of thing—And underneath he paints, pen paints, a small poem, just a line or two, capturing the essence—Like Heraclitus."

"Mmm." said Cathleen. "Well, you've seen them and I haven't. Sounds a funny pair of bedfellows though—"

"I suppose they are," Rosamund had her doubts too. "All a bit made-up. Still, it does seem to jell, and that's the test. His work is much sought after in France, or so he says. He does collage too. And he's formidably clever." She came to the crux. "He's a knock-out, quite beautiful, all black velvet suit and long white fingers."

"Handsome, but not much of an artist?" asked Cathleen. "Caravaggio—"

"Oh for heaven's sake. Who's as good as Caravaggio? Or Tiepolo. Or Uccello. Or Vermeer. Or Rembrandt. Or even Magritte. But he has flair."

"Are you in love with him?" Cathleen dared to ask.

"Good heavens no! At least, only a soupçon. We all sit mooning over him while he talks about the Pre-Columbians— We all vie for his attention like the veriest schoolkids. He's got a

123

smashing Greek girl he's living with or married to, or something. It's a lost cause." Her husky voice trailed into nothing.

Cathleen looked up from the long kimono she was ironing: this year it was all long dresses for Rosamund, practically fancy-dress. Her eyes flickered away from her mother's. Was this the rainbow and the lightning bolt? Or just a final adolescent crush, by way of wind up. In her bones or in her fibres, or whatever place it is—(Harry Cohn kept his antennae in his fanny, she remembered irrelevantly)—somewhere, somehow she knew that this was the one who would beckon to Rosamund; and she would follow.

"Artists," she said lightly, holding the scarlet silk sash up to the light. "Look, there's a little moth-hole—or maybe it's a tear—Artists make better lovers than husbands. They are really only committed to their work. They pluck so wantonly and throw away so carelessly."

"What did you say?" Rosamund was shocked. "They *what*? Oh, they *pluck*!" Rosamund burst out laughing. "My good little mother and that wicked word—I couldn't believe my ears! It was as if the sun climbed down to take a breather." After one nonplussed moment, Cathleen laughed too.

It was Easter. The Easter ceremonies are outmoded now; a mockery even; however the holiday is acceptable. Rosamund did not come home for Easter. She had decided to stay in the dump near the University with half a dozen other students. So much work to be done, it was really piling up now. And there was so much going on at the moment, films, the workshops, marvellous music, Peter Sculthorpe's new opera, oh, everything—

"Of course," said Cathleen. "It's your last year, make the most of it."

But she missed the bright fall of hair, the gusts of laughter, the tirades and tenderness of her headstrong girl. I have to get used to doing without her, she told herself. I have to shape another life for myself. She has almost finished devouring me, but there is enough left (I think, I hope) to begin again. Look at the terrible things people have to get used to: that poor lad in the village tumbled head first off his motor bike, now forever imprisoned in his wheelchair. Betty Jackson's son, forever hooked on drugs. Christina, that lovely girl, dead and gone. People have to put up with all manner of deprivations. Mavis Johnson, her husband walking out on her after eighteen good years, leaving her flat for a girl hardly older than his daughter.

"A trollop!" Mavis had cried violently. "No pretence of love, just sex pure and simple!" Or impure and complicated, thought Cathleen. In the staffroom they all commiserated with poor Mavis, away now on sick leave; all sighed that men were such babies, any little tart could pull the wool over their eyes.

"I guess though that's only if they want to be fooled," said Cathleen. "People have a way of going for what they want in life."

They rounded on her, those clued-up teachers. What did she know of the great world outside Alcheringa.

"You are so unworldly," someone said.

"I saw her back away from the porn magazines down at the newsagents," said someone else.

"That girl Jack took off with, she wears pants with the gussets cut out, Mavis told me." Meg was Mavis's best friend.

"How does she know?" asked Cathleen.

"He had a pair of them in his hip pocket," said Meg. "But don't say I told you, Mavis'd kill me."

They all chewed their sandwiches, before the next round. Cathleen drank her tea, and listened. She didn't want to be drawn in to discussions on the Last Tango in Paris or the Clockwork Orange or any old-hat shock movies. My daughter is truly liberated, she wanted to say: not just pretending. My daughter and her friends know about Now in life and Now in art, not the stale old stuff you're dredging up. And I can't keep up with your slick talk, but I know about passion and about betrayal as none of you will ever know. Her silence provoked them.

"Come down from your ivory tower, Cathy. You've only got to follow the media to know about the ghastly things happening every day."

Cathleen looked from one face to another, each one firm-set in a mould of acceptance, so different from the questing passionate faces of the young. Their concern was pseudo at best she thought; a mixture of indifference and gloating.

"They always did, didn't they?" She put her cup down. "But

125

as for our particular form of mess—well, I don't read the papers much, and I don't watch the news on television. I hate hearing about all the violence and rapacity. Besides—the solutions seem so simple—"

Simple? They all stared at her.

"Explain yourself," said Meg.

"Well, there's enough in the world for everyone, isn't there?" she asked. "It's all mixed up with getting and spending, isn't it? All these useless commodities we're exhorted to buy—If every woman was sterilized after two children, and cars taken away except for community service, necessary trucking, doctors—not carting face-creams and fancier cars and gimmicks. And boys had to use up their energies in National Service, conservation and irrigation, all that, and porn magazines exiled, and bad criminals executed, because what good are they in the world anyway—And if we truly learned to love our neighbours, or at least tolerate them, and remember we all started the same way and we're all going the same place—"

They goggled. Then they derided. "You are so unworldly, Cathleen. What about big business?"

"Leave me my Volvo, I've just finished paying for it." That was Meg.

Cathleen flushed. "That's what I meant," she said under her breath. "Anyway I can't see why if nations can harness their energies for war, they can't do it for peace."

"Are you a communist, Cathleen?"

"I'm not anything," said Cathleen, rattled by the accusation in all the faces that were turned on her. "All I think is, we made our way out of the slime, we made families and tribes and nations—so why can't we make one world?"

The bell rang. They scraped back their chairs, relieved to be summoned. It was getting too near the bone: pat-ball, chit-chat, these are topics fit for luncheon in the staffroom.

"You are so unworldly, Cathleen," they sighed, as they went out.

"So impassioned!" mocked the owner of the Volvo, showing her claws.

A letter came, bidding Cathleen to make an appointment at the bank, to discuss her finances. Some bonds had matured; it was necessary to re-allocate the money.

Rosamund was away, there was no one to advise her. Not that Rosamund, with her profligate disregard of money, would be much help. And as long as Cathleen had enough to fill her needs, money did not loom large in her life, either. She paid her superannuation, took what she needed from her salary for living, and left the rest for her bank manager to worry about: his job. She had a small savings account, but the rest, a fairly substantial rest, these days, she simply paid over and forgot about. Now she had to make decisions.

At the bank she was ushered in with impressement, treated like a VIP. The manager, all beams, was the one who had advised her five years before, when she had finished paying for the house, and found that she had money to spare. She was amazed when he told her how her savings had grown.

"Forty thousand dollars! Why, that's a fortune!" She was sure he had made a mistake.

"We don't make mistakes in this bank," he stated firmly, not very amused. Then he relented and smiled, "Well, I did right by your money, Mrs. Bell. Now, what are we going to do with your capital? Water Board? Electricity Commission? Both quite sound. Interest not enormous, but very stable investments. Or there are our own interest bearing deposits. Safe as a bank, you know," he said, laughing at his own little sally.

"No." Cathleen held up the leaflet she had picked up from the desk outside. "I'd like you to split it in two, half for my daughter and half for me. This eight per cent investment one."

He blanched. "Oh but that's too generous. The young must wait, you know. Give her a thousand or two."

"No. She'll be twenty one soon. She needs it now, not when she's forty. And I want to see her have it now, not when I'm dead."

"What will she do with it?" he asked helplessly, at a loss. "Mrs. Bell, I must tell you that you're making a terrible mistake."

"I should think she'll give most of it away," said Cathleen proudly. "To somebody or some cause that needs it more than she does. She's not mercenary at all, she's just about the least greedy person in the world. I wouldn't be strong enough to do it, but she will. But perhaps she'll use a little bit of it for a trip—"

He was bewildered. "To Europe?"

"To Europe and to Iceland. And perhaps she'll tuck a few hundred away."

"Oh dear." He shook his head as if to clear it. "Can't I possibly persuade you—?"

"No. But because I'm older than she is, and not so resilient any more, please will you look after the other half for me. Sometimes I think I won't be able to teach forever—well, that would be plenty for me to live on." She smiled at him, grateful for his skilful manipulation, grateful and amazed.

"Little lady," he said, heavily gallant, getting to his feet. "You really need a man to look after all that money. And after you, too." he added. He looked as if he wouldn't mind taking on the job himself. "You're heart's too big for that little body of yours. Are you still living in the house on the waterfront?"

Cathleen knew what was coming. His last word gave him away. "Yes. Goodbye. Thank you again."

He would not be silenced. "You're sitting on a goldmine," he said. "They could put twenty units on that block—they'd give you one to live in as part of the deal."

"Never," said Cathleen. "Over my dead body."

"You are very unworldly, Mrs. Bell." His voice floated after her.

Oh shut up, she said, under her breath.

15

Unworldly Cathleen might be, but blind she was not. It was clear to her that Rosamund had a lover. When she came home for a day or two here and there, her eyes met Cathleen's then glanced off. Her conversation was the merest badinage, as if she feared that to open her lips would unlock a door which no one else must be allowed to enter. She divested her room of all its treasures, as she never had done before. On the old treadle machine she sewed cushions of beautiful faded colours; old-rose silk, cream satin patterned with roses, black brocade scrolled with silver and rosy chrysanthemums.

She ironed them herself, and draped them over the chair backs to admire them. She borrowed Cathleen's travelling bag so that they would not be crushed. "It's called Rose Street, did I tell you? So I've made it all very couleur de rose, my room, I painted the walls a sort of silvery green, like a rose-leaf, and I bought a gorgeous sleazy old rose satin bedspread from the flea market. Guaranteed to be jumping with bed-bugs. And sometimes I have real roses there," she said shyly. Before Cathleen could answer she changed the subject. "Must be prepared! An hour in the bus with a full bladder is torture, let me tell you." She banged the bathroom door to show that the discussion was closed.

Cathleen hesitated: she had some rose soap, French, most subtly scented, that she longed to add to the trousseau. She did not dare: it would have been branded intrusion. Instead she stroked the dark leather, such an old bag, her mother's wedding-case, the locks still strong but speckled with rust. Take care of her, she implored silently, importuning any saint who might guard girls too rash and loving-hearted.

"How's your Desportes?" she dared to ask, picking up her embroidery, accepting the light kiss of farewell.

The guarded note in Rosamund's voice told Cathleen what she knew already: the other inhabitant of the rose-coloured world.

"Louis? Oh alright, I guess. His girl-friend's gone back to Greece."

"I thought she was his wife."

Rosamund shrugged. "What's the difference? Either two people are committed to each other, or not. A bit of mumbo-jumbo in a church doesn't alter anything, does it? Unless they happen to believe in it?"

"Which is she? His girl friend or his wife? Rosamund?"

The girl moved impatiently. "Look, I've no idea. He collects ladies pretty freely about him. Why are we talking about him anyway?" Her voice trailed off into silence.

Cathleen retreated, conscious that she had set foot in a country where she had no right to stray. "Goodbye then," she said. "Be happy darling. Will you be home for vacation?"

"No I won't mum. Sorry. I'm staying in town to finish some paintings. I've got half a dozen daubs I'm working on. Desportes arranged a little exhibition for me in Glebe, at least he's trying to get it lined up. It's a place they use for University—not a bad little joint. Oh, that reminds me, I want to take these two back—All Loving—where is it, and the Fairy-tale thing—" She clapped them quite roughly together and tucked them under her arm. Bag in one hand, pictures in one arm, tall and blond, she nodded a grave farewell. "Don't worry if you don't hear from me mamma mia. Just go on cultivating your garden, eh?"

Weeks passed. No Rosamund. As autumn went over, reddening the rhus, a scrawled postcard came, proclaiming her to be still alive, painting like crazy (most of them crap). There was no address, visitors were not of the essence. She needn't have worried, thought Cathleen, I'd rather be holed up with a porcupine than drop in on her, unasked.

In June she telephoned. "That you, mum? You sound very fady. Must be a bad connection. Listen, it's on all this week, my shivoo."

"So soon?"

"I'll give you the address. Don't expect anything too grand will you? It's that community project house that all the Fine Arts people use. Pretty squalid outside, but it serves the purpose. Lets us give our stuff an airing—"

"Shall I see you?" asked Cathleen. It's been months, she wanted to cry out.

There was a moment's silence. "Why not?" said her daughter's voice. "Come about one. I'll look out for you.

Tomorrow? Right."

Like the prudent pig in the story, Cathleen came at twelve. She could hardly contain her excitement as the bus ate up the miles between Alcheringa and the room in the city where her girl's secret life lay spread out for all to see. A honeyed tongue he must have, this fellow to persuade a girl so inward to line up and display all her wealth of visions. Although, as she said, when she finished them she was done with them. "Thank God," she had added fervently. "That's the only solution to the artist's predicament. Done, they're done with."

Behind iron spikes and an oblong of tan-bark the house waited. The door was open, propped back by a lump of plaster in the shape of a cobra. No, it was a phallus. Cathleen swallowed. All doors had been removed from the interior, the walls painted cream. In the ante-room stood a long bench, slatted. Looks as if it's waiting for prisoners, thought Cathleen, wanting to laugh, but composing her face into lines of reverence, as one waiting for the communion wafer.

From the chambers within drifted the sound of coughing and snatches of conversation. Diffidently Cathleen went through the first archway and strove to melt into the throng.

Some hope! She was almost the only person without a beard, certainly the only one not encased in tight jeans—Long hair, tight T-shirts strained across flat chests: only their smooth cheeks singled the two girls out from the swarm of boys. Boys and girls, they were shuffling into a room which had once been a parlour. And there, on the walls behind the curtain of cigarette smoke were Rosamund's paintings, glowing like small separate fires against the pale walls.

Unframed Exposition, said the catalogue tacked up on the wall; one to serve all-comers, apparently.

Cathleen stood still, and tried to distance herself. Were they good? Were they bad? She had no way of telling. "Impact," she heard somebody behind her mutter, and she seized on the word gratefully. Everything Rosamund did had impact, had flair. There was her H.S.C. painting of a woman turning into a tree, a woman past youth, deeply sad. Her skin was like bark. She is turning into a tree because she is finished with life, thought Cathleen. Why, her face is mine ten years from now.... On the far wall was a cave of blue, but the cave was the sky. The cross

131

on the ground was a kite-man, spreadeagled, crucified; and the figures clustered around him were birds, magpies, digging their beaks into his mangled flesh.

"Pretty strong stuff," she heard a boy say. "Of course Rosie's strong on revenge."

Cathleen peeped at him, but he turned his back. He was scanning the next picture, a happy one, thank goodness. A long chain of girls, all contained in the symbol of infinity, each one's head supporting the upside down one above. Upright, upside down, upright, upside down, it went; all the faces were the same, but subtly different, blue eyes became brown, became hazel. Growing, it was called; the chain of life. At one moment it looked like a daisy-chain; at another a string of beads.

"I'm dazzled," said a boy with a ginger beard and a shaven head. "Rosie's been hiding her light under a bushel."

"It's demented! She's demented! Did you see the one called the Place of Delight? Everybody up to something unsavoury?"

"They're pretty powerful. M-More vision than technique," said a thin boy with glasses. "Still—technique's not too hard to come by—"

"They're crazy!" His companion, a pretty girl with a spiteful face took his arm. "Come on, Patrick, I've got better things to do."

"They're beautiful!" said Cathleen, in indignation.

The boy with a stammer smiled at her. "You're so r-r-right," he said. "Go through. The best is yet to be."

So she went through, questing. "All Loving" was there. The three crows and the casuarinas were there. One of a shack quite overgrown with sunflowers and fennel, caught surely at the moment before it sighed and collapsed. The rabbit ladies were there, celebrated in all their idiosyncracy. Two boys stopped and murmured approbation.

Cathleen progressed. Before her, stretched a long wall that held two pictures, two only. She gagged. They were horrible, sickening: only a depraved mind could have created them. Three boys bounded in, and stopped short in adulation. One of them had been there before; a glutton for punishment, he had come back with his friends. Cathleen looked at them because she couldn't bear to look at the pictures. They were performing all sorts of mumbo-jumbo with their hands; they stepped in close; they backed away; they surveyed with narrowed eyes. They bravoed and nodded their sanction, and they bounded out.

Cathleen stood alone. She looked from one picture to the other, from the black to the red, and she loathed them equally, feared them equally. Rosamund, her daughter had painted these celebrations of despair and violence. She stood transfixed, her mouth ajar.

"Symbolism," she heard someone say behind her. "Very fin de siècle. But she brings it off quite triumphantly, don't you think?" Two portly middleaged gentlemen with University accents and safari suits, were standing in judgement, preparing to pronounce.

"Very slight, the others—but these are exciting, don't you agree?"

His friend agreed. "I was not unimpressed with the fairy-tale picture. A fresh vision. Enigmatic but fresh, wouldn't you say? One remembers one's own childhood as if it were yesterday." They moved on, there was a little annexe beyond.

Had they ever been children? Exciting they said. But these are horrible, horrible, thought Cathleen, forcing herself to look.

La Perduta Gente it was called: the most simple and most despairing picture she had ever looked at. It was a black square, a great black square holding a child, thrown back at the moment of birth. Or was it a wizened old man, consigned to space?

On his back he lunged towards her, his mouth a cavern of despair, his flesh a grisly rotting green, his flung-out hands seeking an anchor, but finding nothing. The thrust-out legs and feet had left their springboard behind, were lost in a sea of blackness. It is a fine picture, thought Cathleen, taking a grip on herself, but oh! it is horrible!

The other one was worse. The Heart in the Casket. All those years ago she had confiscated that cruel story, tried to forget it. But Rosamund had remembered; and she had re-created it:

A girl with the face of an angel and hair bright as gold sat on a grassy knoll, her white skirts spread about her. Above her head grew a tree, thick massed with white flowers, with angel's trumpets. On her lap the girl held a casket, and in her hands she held a heart. Fresh blood dripped through her fingers, and stained the white stuff of her dress. The last rays of the sun gilded her hair, lit up her face with an unearthly shining, lit up her expression of indescribable glee. Shadowy in the dark trees, her lover waited for her. In her exultation she let him wait, while she gloated over her rival's heart.

Cathleen turned away, unable to look at it. Her head swam, her legs felt weak. She found her way out to the bench and sat down. There were other pictures to see, but she had seen enough.

Have I spawned a monster, she wondered, and waited, quite numb, for the monster she had spawned.

At one o'clock, on the dot, Rosamund bounced in, very high. She was rather pale and hollow-cheeked, but happy.

"Well, are you pleased?" she asked, her voice rather gruff, as it always was when she felt shy.

"I think you have immense talent. More than I realized," said Cathleen. "Some of them look unfinished."

"Of course. They were preliminary designs, really. Like my cheek to put them in. Did you like the Place of Delight?" she asked wickedly.

"I didn't get as far as that. I stopped short at the one about the heart in the casket. And the other awful one, the baby."

"A space-man, really," Rosamund corrected her. "But a baby too. And of course an old man—You no lika da nitty-gritty mamma mia?"

"They shocked me," said Cathleen. "And why did you paint that terrible girl, gloating like that. With your face—"

"Well, it's a long story," said Rosamund, signalling to a chorus of new arrivals. "See, I thought I'd practically be capable of cutting out anyone's heart if she kept me from—"

"But the story doesn't go like that. The whole story is the way the son kills his mother, and the bleeding heart cries out to him in love—"

"Oh, it's a pretty good story," said Rosamund thoughtfully. "There's a dozen truths embedded in it. There's a Jewish version I believe, with a possessive mother. You pay your money and you take your choice. I happened to want to paint it this way. Of course, all the good myths have many facets. Interpret it as you please."

"I can see only one way," said Cathleen. "So don't dazzle me with words, Rosamund."

"Since when were you dazzled with words?" asked Rosamund. "Sorry they disturbed you. Come and see The Place of Delight, and get shook up all over again. I promise you'll come out all of a doodah."

"Never," said Cathleen stoutly. "I have supped full of horrors."

"Alright. Come over to Manning and have a cup of tea. I've got something to give you. A communication."

Over at Manning, they had to wait in a queue for their tea. Rosamund was much acclaimed, and very blasé about it.

"They don't know much about it, most of them. Some do, though. Look at that pig Sophie Mosca, sitting over there in her sty." She nodded back to a fat little girl who was finishing apple pie and was preparing to tuck into a slice of lemon meringue.

"She's always like that, when she can't decide, she'll take both. Whenever she stops stuffing herself one way, she starts the other." She was deliberately playing dead pan.

They took their tea outside on the grass.

"Gosh you're pale, mum. And that red flannel dress just hangs on you."

"Funny, I was thinking the same about you. Are you still living in Rose Street?"

Rosamund shook her head. "No, I moved out to Paddo with Louis last month. Rose Street was lovely, I'll never forget it, but he had to run the barricade of too many eyes—"

"Do you like it where you are?"

Cathleen was seeking the reason for this pallor and restlessness. Rosamund was jittery, unable to sit still, moving hands and feet restlessly.

"I love it when he's there. I hate it when he's away. It's a concrete jungle. All those anonymous doors. Not a blade of grass."

"Oh," Cathleen was disturbed.

"But it's where he is," said Rosamund, answering the unspoken question. "He can't be too far away from the university. At Christmas we'll find something better. His lease doesn't run out till Christmas."

"Did he live there with his other girl?"

135

Rosamund's cheeks flamed, "Yes," she said briefly. "I hate that. But he's there—so—" She took out a blue envelope. "He wrote you this. I suppose it's baloney," she said. "He's quite a baloney merchant—"

"But—" Cathleen stared at her—

"I can't help myself," said Rosamund, quite desperately. "Any Australian barrow-man is more of a man than he is. He's weak and he's shifty—but when he looks at me over the blue smoke of his pipe—When I hear his voice I—And we talk the same language, he's divinely funny and clever—Oh it's nothing to do with sense!" she said violently, jumping up. "I'm bewitched. And I'm so bloody unhappy that I can't wait for the spell to be broken. Because he must be the biggest bastard in the world."

"I see," said Cathleen. There was nothing she could say. She opened the letter, which was written in French. Chère madame, said the spidery writing. Doggedly she set to work to decipher it: her schoolgirl French was hardly up to the job. It was a proposal of marriage: he was asking for Rosamund's hand.

She ploughed on, battered between the Scylla of his handwriting and the Charybdis of his language. "Oh I can't understand it. Will you translate it? Or I'll have to go home and get a dictionary—"

Rosamund made no attempt to take it. "I don't have to read it to know what it's about. It's a whole lot of bullswhack, for sure. He loves mucking about with words."

"What does that mean, you have the face of his philosophy?" Cathleen had returned to the letter.

"It's hot air mum. He's crazy about the sound of his own voice—But all the girls fall for him, and I'm no exception. He slipped a poem written to me inside my essay when he returned it—An acrostic on my name, Rosamund."

"And you're in love with him?"

"I can't help it. My legs turn to rubber every time I look at him—" Her face was woe-begone.

"Hi Rosie!" called a strine voice, and a boy with the face of a barrowman stood before them. He smiled at Cathleen. "Come and feed."

Rosamund shook her head. "Not hungry." When he lingered, she introduced him. "Mum, this is Tom. Tom, my mother. She's just going home. Come on mum, I'll walk you to the bus."

At the bus-shelter, Cathleen turned to her—"Call me if you need me, darling? Please?—Christina—"

"Oh I'm made of tougher stuff," said Rosamund. "I'll make it to shore. Here's your bus."

Cathleen waited. What else was there to do? Her heart yearned towards her child, no distance away, a world away. Being hurt is part of growing up, deny it and you stunt yourself: true, but hard for a mother to stand by, without wringing her hands. She went sedately through the motions of living; she wondered whether she might take a little sea-voyage in August, kennel the dogs for once, buy a few new clothes. But really, she couldn't be bothered; and besides there might be a summons from Rosamund, and she away. She thought of Christina, alone and abandoned, and she shivered. She thought of going in to the university, to meet Rosamund as she came out of lectures; but she feared rejection. And she had said, Rosamund, that she would paddle her boat to shore. Miserably, stolidly, she went about her tasks. Perhaps next year she would try for promotion. But always, whatever she did, her thoughts flew to her daughter journeying through love's morasses.

In August Rosamund wrote briefly, to say that all was well. In September it would be her birthday. Twenty one years since Cathleen had waited in the house on stilts by the Brisbane River, with the smell of mud and jasmine coming in the window, and that red creeper (she had never found out its name), spilling down the bank to the water. And the baby in her belly stretching out towards life, kicking and punching at the one who impeded it from living.

Cathleen sighed. If Rosamund had a father—but the father she had was all painted out, fled to the bottle for solace, or so Rosamund reported. One of the occupational hazards of artists.

There was no one to help, nothing to do but to wait. So she waited, helpless. But on her birthday, Cathleen vowed, nothing will stop me. I'll take the day off, I've never done it before, they can sack me, I don't care. I'll go in to see her at university, and I'll tell her about the money, and if she shouts me down, then let her, I'll have done something to mark the day. And I'll take her in all the roses from the old bush that blooms all springtime. She went out to see, and yes, it was covered with blossoms and buds and hips, all three at once. Next week, she said to herself, and her heart gave a leap of joy.

It was only the next day when the telephone rang. There was a moment's pause while someone pressed the button, and waited for the coin to drop.

"Mamma. Rosamund here."

"Oh, I was just sitting here thinking about you. It's nearly your birthday."

"I know, mum. I wondered, is there any chance you could come in and meet me in town? Today?"

Cathleen rejoiced. "Yes, of course. Now? Wait, I'll look up the buses. You mean at once, don't you?"

"The sooner the better. I'll be at the bus-stop." She was gone.

Jubilant but jolted, Cathleen looked for the time-table. Her fingers were clumsy and the figures blurred before her. In the end she rushed through a shower, dried herself so skimpily that wet patches sprang out on the back of her linen dress. No matter.

The bus came at last. The long, too-long trip through beaches and suburbs and city was over. From her seat at the top of the bus she saw Rosamund waiting, haunted, in a long black dress. In her haste to reach her child Cathleen stumbled on the steps and half-fell. The bus conductor caught her as she stumbled.

"Careful, lady," he admonished. "You'll come a nasty cropper if you don't watch out."

Rosamund's pale face was touched with gladness when she saw her mother.

"Hi," she said, with a wan smile, cracking hardy as she always did. "By golly, we're a skinny pair, aren't we!"

They went to sit in the little park, with the pigeons roocooing around their feet.

"I hoped to see you for your birthday, Rosamund," said

138

Cathleen. "I wanted to tell you, I've settled a lot of money on you. I don't know how it happened quite, but I'm as rich as Onassis. Nearly," she said, her eyes searching her girl's face.

Rosamund's so-blue eyes answered the unspoken question. "It's all over," she said. "He's a leech as well as a lecher, and he's sucked me dry. Can I come home, mum? Now? Or I'll end up like Christina."

Thank God and the good angels that watched over you, that you didn't, said Cathleen to herself. Aloud, in a quite business-like voice, she said, "Of course. Now, where are your things? Back at the flat? Well, we'll get a taxi, I'll wait at the corner of your street. Is he there now?"

"No, he's out. In somebody else's bed, who cares."

"Right," Cathleen controlled her anger. "Does he know you're leaving?"

"I told him I was. But he didn't really believe me. That's his role, you see. But he asked me, if I go, to leave him my two best paintings, and my little Art Nouveau fire, the copper one. Just to remember me by, you know."

"If I used four-letter words, which I don't," said Cathleen, enraged, "I would say—I don't know what I'd say—Look, there's an empty cab. Come on!"

He importuned Rosamund, her poet who was an artist, who was a skunk. By telephone, by telegram, by letter. Once he came up to Alcheringa, while Cathleen was away at school, and took her walking around the coastline while he begged her to come back to him. She came home shaken but adamant.

"He must have thought there were a few poems still to be got out of me," she said cynically. "He bought me some pink carnations to match my cheeks, and a blue sari to match my eyes. He must be really keen, he's usually got a scorpion in his pocket."

The sari, gleaming turquoise, lay flung across her bed; the carnations gave out their clove scent, unheeded. She gave a small giggle. "One rather funny thing, there were flocks of lorikeets everywhere, and those pink and grey galahs, masses of them. And after about an hour he pointed to one of them and said, Un petit oiseau!—He'd just spied them."

"Did you speak French or English?" Cathleen had often wondered.

139

"Both!" Rosamund laughed and blinked back te..rs. "I used to talk in English, and he'd answer in French. We could both understand perfectly, but could speak our own lingo more spontaneously." She looked down, drooping. "Bear with me, mum. I'll get over it soon."

She worked hard in the garden, taking over Cathleen's tasks. She went in only intermittently to her lectures, but never to his. When he waited outside the lecture-room to see her she brushed past him. And she never stopped sleeping, it seemed. She said that she had hardly slept for three months, he liked to sleep with his arms around her. It was like being curled up with a boa-constrictor, she said. "He slept. I tossed. Everything was done his way, everything. Restaurants, and concrete, and jabber jabber jabber. He bought me an easel, and commanded me to use it for my painting. I hate easels. And I can't paint to order."

Day by day the colour came back to her cheeks. She hacked with fury at the lantana that had taken over the back garden by the bay. She was hungry again, eating ravenously, still thin, but she no longer looked haunted. Her smile was less spontaneous, not the wide dimpled grin of the old days—but she was smiling.

"Convalescing, mum," she said.

"By the time the exams are over, I'll be cured," she said.

Sometimes now she spoke of him. "He'd never really learned to love, only himself. He hated his mother and father." That was one time.

Another: "He had exquisite taste. He was a rotten artist—but a good poet, or goodish. Very intellectual convoluted stuff."

"He was a wonderful lover," said Cathleen, remembering the so long ago. "Weren't you lucky?"

Rosamund looked at her. "How did you know? Was I? Yes, I suppose I was."

16

Squat, shabby, but enduring, it had served its turn, the house next door to Cathleen; now it was levelled, none of it left but a straggle of bricks and a sagging wooden outhouse. Old Miss Murgatroyd, recluse, left over from the fishing village, was three days dead when her brother found her. The house, valuable only for the land fronting the bay, was pulled down. Overnight, it seemed, a sandstock brick and red cedar monster had beanstalked in its place. An interior decorator's van stood before the doorway; and was replaced by a landscape gardener's truck. Each operation left the acreage somewhat more hideous. Now, instead of the comely sweep of rough grass, instead of the great crabapple massy with wisteria, stood a stretch of red gravel, a daunting row of brassy retinosporas, six standard roses, and about a million Hawaiian hibiscus.

"Wow!" said Rosamund, when she came home after six weeks' work at Bathurst. "They pulled out all the stops."

"Didn't they!" As a child Cathleen had been taken to a theatre where a Wurlitzer organ as big as a behemoth rose out of the depths below, complete with organist, who played with matchless ostentation while the multicoloured lights swept over him. Secretly she had thought it marvellous, and the player, with his shiny black hair, as handsome as a prince. But her mother had pronounced the entertainment very vulgar, as of course it was. Now, looking at the house next door, Cathleen remembered the organ.

"Does the lady live up to her domicile?" asked Rosamund, leaning against the knotty thongs of a turpentine trunk, folding her arms, watching her mother hose the violets. She rubbed a sprig of eau de cologne mint between her palms. "This is a good smelly kind of garden," she approved. She had her bag at her feet, stuffed fat with books or dirty washing or both.

Cathleen was happy. It seemed that she had come to stay. "I haven't seen her. She drives one of those snappy Italian cars, and he drives a big black one like a hearse."

"Who does the garden?"

"A young man. A very decorative young man with beautiful red hair, who knows nothing in the world about plants. He cut all the buds off the camellias, they won't flower next season now, not that it matters in that cesspool of a garden. He went around pruning everything, willy-nilly. He cleans the pool too, I think."

"A pool yet? Where is it?"

"Right down on the bay, I think." The mention of a pool triggered off memory. "By the way, did Florence finish the year?" Florence had an impressive record of failures and muddled courses. "Gerty said she swore that this time she'd make it."

Rosamund shook her head. "No, she says she's taken a sabbatical. She didn't come back from Italy with the other kids. You know, I told you about the Fine Arts tour they arranged before Trinity. She was having too much fun in Rome to leave." She picked up her bag. "I might just look the gardener over one day."

"He's very ignorant," said Cathleen. "He says things like mischievious and he talks in that rhyming slang, Noah's ark for shark, and so on. I heard him chatting to the postman, another good-looking young slob. I was weeding the strawberry bed, and they were propping up the gate, one on each side, for half an hour." She turned off the hose. "Come inside, darling, you look famished."

"I think you're a snob, mamma mia. A twee little snob." Rosamund was indignant. "Pretty low of you to pick on somebody for his accent. You can't imagine how sick I am of university snobs and skites. Kafka this, Merz that, Joyce old-hat, someone else new-hat, Whitehead outmoded—a word for everything. If they could hear me spitting venom now they'd call me ignivomous. Vomiting fire, you know," she added.

"Thank you. I'm familiar with the word."

"Sorry. You looked rattled. I'm so bloody sick of words, I could do with a bit of hush."

"He'll fill the bill," Cathleen joined Rosamund in the easy laughter of two people who have weathered years together.

Rosamund smacked her lips. "I'm in the very mood for a bit of roughneck courting. It's entirely too civilized, what I've been subjected to in the last years." As the days went past she kept her vigil. Soon the young gardener found it imperative to work in the area where the properties converged, before the sandstock brick wall began its march to the bay.

"Didn't they have enough bricks left to finish the wall?" she asked cheekily. She was wearing slacks and gum-boots, her hair in a long plait: her usual attire when she used the motor-mower. She hated its noise and stink and vibration; when she could locate a strong hand-mower she was going to change over. She turned off the throttle and dimpled at him: her drawcard.

Soon she was carrying him a cup of tea and hot scones, and smiling at his jokes. With his height and his blazing red hair he made her look fragile and pastel-coloured. They did not talk much, but a great deal of laughter came from the arc of ground where they were pretending to work.

One day, one Thursday, he stalked up the path, crestfallen. Rosamund came to the door to greet him.

"I just come to say goodbye. The lady give me the sack."

"Oh!" Rosamund drew a breath. "Come in. Don't be silly, of course you're not too dirty. Look at me! What happened?"

All ears, Cathleen pretended to be busy with the lemon cheese she was making.

He was discomfited. Pressed, he gave his answer. "She said I spent too much time talking over the fence."

Now Rosamund was the one discomfited. "Oh, I *am* sorry. Will you be able to get another job?"

"Who cares? I was only filling in time anyway, getting a bit of money together for the farm."

"Farm? A real farm?" Rosamund moved closer. "You didn't say you had a farm."

"It's my grandfather's old place. Way down past Nowra. Gee, it's pretty down there. Wish I could take you," he ventured.

"So do I," breathed Rosamund.

"Would you come? We go down most weekends. The whole family. I wish you'd come, gee—"

"When?"

"What about comin' home for tea, and we'll go to a show?" A red-headed Australian larrikin, pushy but shy, he leaned towards her. His glance was a caress.

Cathleen cleared her throat. They moved apart.

The girl was the first to recover. "Mum, this is Phil. He works—or used to work—in the garden next door." She took off.

"You did terrible things to that defenceless garden," said Cathleen. "I don't think it will ever recover."

"What's the diff?" He shrugged his shoulders, wide but bony under his faded blue shirt. "I was only stackin' it away so's I can leave the rat-race and go down south."

"What sort of a farm is it?" asked Cathleen.

"Used to be a mixed farm. Me grandfather died and it got run-down. Soon I'm gonna get it goin' again."

"All alone?" asked Cathleen. "It sounds a big job."

"Me father an' brothers'll help me out." He was shifting from one foot to the other. Plainly he didn't think much of putting in time with older women.

Rosamund, scrubbed clean, her hair in wet tendrils around her cheeks, was back. She was wearing a blue denim dress and sandals. "Let's go," she said. And they went.

In the days that followed she was always coming and going, bringing back reports from a country alien to her. He lived, the ex-gardener, in a house on the river near Como, with five brothers and a devastating old father, and a mother who was only a cypher. "Six sons! Cross my heart! There are seven cars parked around their place. The youngest is still at school. Also four motor-bikes." Three of the boys were dark and two were fair, and one, Phillip, was red. They worked in all kinds of nonesuch places, like Paddy's market, and oyster-leases and oh yes, one was at university, one was a plumber—

"Really, there were so many faces around the table that I don't know who does what. We went to a spy movie. It was fun."

"But Rosamund, he's almost illiterate. You couldn't possibly contemplate—"

"He's got a farm," said Rosamund. "They're country people, really. He's longing to go back. They hate the rat-race."

"No doubt." said her mother. "Seven cars to one house. They sound homesick for Eden."

"Shut your trap!" The violence of her tone showed Rosamund's unease. "Anyway, we're all going down on Friday. He's been working all around Australia to get enough money for the farm."

144

"Bludging," Cathleen corrected her, "He's bludged all around Australia, you mean." She was sick and tired of sloppy young teachers, sloppy young labourers, sloppy young salesmen.

"Who asked you? I wish I hadn't told you about him. I only did because I was sorry for your miserable pittance of a life."

Cathleen bridled, "Soon you'll be on your way, and I'll live for myself again."

"Do that, will you? It's too much of a bind to have you living for me. I might be on my way sooner than you think. Mind if I use the oven?"

She set to work and made two enormous square cakes, one thick with raisins, one with dates and walnuts. By the time she had finished cleaning up the mess she was over her paddy.

"He's looking for a wife, you know. He reckons I bowled him over. Who knows, I might like it on a farm. Painting and looking after the animals."

Innocent Rosamund, still ardent, still believing in Paradise. With her cakes and her rough farm clobber she set off on her new quest. Phillip came to collect her in his campmobile, to take her back to Como to catch forty winks as he said, before they set off in the wee small hours.

"You look a very engaging pair," said Cathleen, by way of truce: squaring off, as he would call it.

The young man didn't like her. "Talk English, why don't you?" he muttered.

Rosamund looked startled. She frowned, then smiled. "My mother was reared on Shakespeare," she explained.

"Shakespeare," he scoffed. "Ready, Rosie? Come on, I'm sick of hangin' around, honey."

Cathleen watched the van turn the corner. She sighed. Thank goodness nobody's making me get up cock-crow, she thought. Yes, I really am getting old. Rosamund is no sooner finished with one enthusiasm than she throws herself into another. It must be nice though to be going off somewhere or staying put somewhere with a man who is in love with you. It was the one dream she had never quite put behind her. Still, when she looked at the marriages around her, the women reporting quarrels about money and children and everything in the world, she thought that perhaps Rosamund was right, that men weren't domestic creatures, by and large, and that no marriage could survive unless the two people were going the same way. Yoked by interest or necessity, as she put it. So I'd better start counting my blessings, Cathleen thought, and leave well alone. But just in case, I'll hold myself in readiness: to live with the thought of never-again is too dispiriting.

Days passed; and then a week. And Rosamund was back, the idyll over. She was not disposed to dwell on the events (or non-events, as she called them) of her week among the haystacks. The beach was quite unspoiled, the water like crystal, the sands white, the hills—oh yes—

"Did they like your cakes?" asked her mother.

"What? Oh yes, what d'you reckon? Everything I did was a great hit. Except with Bob's girl-friend, she came too, and her nose was out of joint. I was Queen of the Bikies."

"Why didn't you like it then?"

"Because I was literally that, queen of the bikie gang. They had four motor-bikes altogether, and they kept roaring up and down the hills. The birds were scared and so was I. My bum was black and blue from bouncing on the pillion."

Cathleen hid her amusement. "What about the farm? All the animals?"

"That's yet to come. The only animal I could see was Phil, and by the end of the time he looked like one of those red cows, moo, moo. The old farmhouse was lovely, and the paddocks. But—"

"On the way down they ran over a kangaroo. They were speeding. Phil had to get out and shoot it. Oh, it was horrible, its mate was hopping about in the headlights, all distracted. He pulled it into the bushes at the side of the road. I hated it." She started to cry, tears that she had kept inside her for a week. She sat up and blew her nose. "Funny, isn't it, how some people kill for fun. You either like it or hate it, I guess. Oh mum, don't look so upset. It's all over, the crows have picked its bones by now. It was—What's wrong?"

Cathleen was swaying. She sat down with a thump. "I don't know. I just felt faint."

"Right." said Rosamund. "I'm taking you to the doctor. I've always thought you were far too listless. All those colds."

"Last year when you were away I had one cold after another. And this year I was sick, really sick."

146

"Why didn't you tell me?"

"I got better in the end. And there was so much happening to you that it didn't seem right to bother you."

"Oh, mamma mia, you're so damned unselfish and long-suffering that I don't know whether to kiss you or kill you." Rosamund was anxious. "Come on, comb your hair and we'll go. No sense in waiting. It's probably just anaemia. Did you get those iron pills? I told you to, remember?"

"No," said Cathleen. "I thought it was just age."

The doctor took one look at Cathleen's finger-nails, turned back her eye-lids, and said he'd send her for blood tests, but he didn't need to. "Are your periods heavy?" he asked.

"Yes. Until the last few months."

"Very simple case of blood loss. Often happens to females in their reproductive years. We'll give you a couple of B12 injections and a course of iron pills, and you'll be a new woman in no time." Tall and spare, very assured, made wise by years on the job, he began to prepare a syringe. Cathleen sat, limply waiting his pleasure. Once, she thought, I'd have day-dreamed about him. Now I'm just too tired.

There was a sound of scuffling, and Rosamund stood at the door, a receptionist, ousted, behind her.

"I came in to see what's wrong with my mother." Her voice was light, her face apprehensive.

The doctor almost dropped the syringe. He started to be vexed, then he looked into the fair face of the intruder. He began to smile. "Nothing to worry about. Just extremely anaemic. Probably her haemoglobin's been down for years. Very simply rectified. Well, you're a very good daughter," he said, advancing towards Cathleen while he bestowed his smiles on Rosamund. "I really don't know how she kept on working."

"Iron will," said Rosamund briefly.

17

When she looked back, it hardly seemed possible to Cathleen, how she had wasted these last years. They had slipped through her limp fingers, while her energies dwindled away. Lethargy begets lethargy; habit enslaves. The malaise had spread from her body to her spirit.

Now, a month later, day by day her strength was surging back. She was eager to start each day's living; more than ready to quit her bed. She had intended to hire someone to paint the house; instead she set to work herself with sheets of coarse sandpaper, preparing the timber as she had seen the house-painters do when last they came.

"Wonders will never cease," Rosamund remarked. "It's nice to see you so full of verve. Listen, mum, how about using a bit of it on a tramp to Granada. They're on the job there too, you know, those advocates of progress. It's being whacked up into a dozen blocks."

"Oh no!" Cathleen made a face and put down the sandpaper. "It had to come, I suppose, an acre and a half—more—As my bank manager would say, they were sitting on a gold mine."

"Well, by this time next year it'll be nothing but a memory. Let's go and look our fill before it's too late." When Cathleen hesitated she spoke brusquely. "Come on then. I can't wait all day."

Cathleen gathered up her tools of trade. It's alright for me to wait all day long, all year long, even, she thought rebelliously. But now I've started a job of my own, I still have to come when you whistle.

Rosamund was impatient to go. "Don't come if you don't want, then. But after all you've got your whole life to paint the house."

As they walked, Cathleen ruminated: she spoke the exact truth, my daughter. I have my whole life to do any little tasks I set myself, all of them piffling, all of them self-imposed. I could go abroad if I wanted to, but I don't want to. In fact there's nothing in the world I have to do, or need to do, but I'm burning up inside.

"Hey mum, slow down," called Rosamund. "I can't keep up

with you. You're walking as if the devil's driving you."

"He is," Cathleen answered her. "All that new energy you injected me with, and I've no idea how to use it. No wonder adolescent boys hell around. They must be on fire! Now I understand why you were such a termagant."

"Thank you. Well, you'll just have to find some way to harness it, won't you.?"

They had reached their goal. Round one bend after another, round the curve of the crescent, up to the crest of the hillock; and Granada stood before them.

"It's a period-piece," said Rosamund. "Or getting that way. Architecturally it's not up to much, just an example of Hollywood Spanish. Nineteen thirty five, would you say?"

"My year," Cathleen realized aloud. "I was born in nineteen thirty five. Yes, it belongs to the old State theatre and the brilliantined organist, in the time between the depression and the war." They peered through the broken panes at the octagonal lobby, stood on tiptoe to peep through the kitchen window. "I daresay it was luxury incarnate then," she said. "I think a doctor built it, a Macquarie street specialist as my mother used to call them. Now, of course, the specialists are everywhere."

Downstairs there was a billiard table, heavily carved, ornate. "The gentlemen came down here to tell their dirty stories then, I suppose. Hey, mum, what are you doing?"

Cathleen had propped up a ladder and was climbing up to inspect the balcony at close quarters. She was up quite high: it felt deliciously unstable. "It's nice up here," she called down. "The balcony must be sun-washed all day long, and with this little bit of extra height you can see Bear Island."

"Please come down," Rosamund begged, "Look, the ladder's got borers. It's nearly collapsed. You'll break your pelvis, you silly old goat."

Hastily Cathleen climbed down. She followed Rosamund's gaze across the bay.

"It must have been beautiful once. Look, you can see what it must have been like in the old days," said Rosamund, dreaming. "That road to the hotel would have been dirt, and a few shabby useful houses, a sprinkle of them. And the hotel was a wooden lean-to, not grand at all. And you looked down from here over sheets of bougainvillea to an absolutely clear undefiled stretch of blue. Or the rain pelted down, and blotted out the hills." She shivered luxuriously.

"Nothing lasts forever," said Cathleen, "you can't keep anything to yourself. And it's still pretty nice, I think." Her eyes skimmed over the huddle of motor-boats at the petrol-bowser, and sought instead the white sails weaving over blue water, and the untamed thickets of bushland on the farther shore. From here their own house was invisible, tucked away in one of the lesser bays.

Rosamund was more grieved than indignant. Her face mourned for this pleasant holding decimated, but she no longer spent her forces on useless diatribes. She turned away. "Come round here when you're ready. I want to show you something."

Cathleen lingered. She looked her fill before she rounded the corner, to find Rosamund enthroned in a stone alcove under a canopy of wisteria, which she had tossed aside to reach within. Her dress and hair were thick with fallen flowers: the wisteria was blooming out of season.

"Look!" she gestured. "That was a lily-pond once upon a time." In the flagged semi-circle before her feet was a dried-out semi-circular pond, now only a receptable for beer cans and cigarette butts. She pointed to a white square in the ground. "Look at that, will you?" Cathleen looked at the surveyor's peg, set with hideous accuracy between the curved stone seat and the pool. "Aren't they unspeakable?" Rosamund groaned. "They gave the pool to one block, and the exedra to another. They were planned as an entity, you know."

Cathleen moved restlessly. What was done was done. "People have to live somewhere. Why shouldn't a dozen people enjoy this pleasant prospect?"

Rosamund glared. "Alright, you're so bloody high-minded. Why don't you sell your land for units?"

"That's different," said Cathleen, bridling.

"Yes, it's always different when it's yourself," Rosamund jeered. "Not that I want you to sell it, I'd kill you if you did— You've got to have space to move about and breathe."

"The bank manager said I was sitting on a gold mine. He advised me to sell out, in fact he gave me masses of advice."

That reminded Rosamund. "Look, mum, I don't want your money. You worked for it. I didn't."

"It worked for itself," cried Cathleen. "It was disgusting, really, I just put it in the bank and they made it grow. I thought you'd know a good way to dispose of it."

"I'll give it some thought. I'll take my fare—you wanted to give me that, didn't you? And I'll find some really worthy recipient for the rest. You might find some guy or some cause to invest in yourself, mum. You've been frozen in a dream. Fairy-tales and dreams, let's vow to be done with them."

"Strange," said Cathleen. "There's really nothing I've got to do now. You're reared. I can work or not, as I please, my blessed—cursed—thrift has fixed that up for me." I feel stranded, she wanted to say. There's nothing in the world I'm needed for now, nobody whose eyes will light up when I come in, once you go. "I wish I—oh, I don't know what I wish!" she cried aloud, and she picked up the beer can at her feet and hurled it into the pool, to clank against the others.

"Well!" Rosamund was tickled. "You'll have to find some cause to spend yourself on. Maybe you'll open a play-centre for deprived children? No? Or take in a foster child?"

"I've thought of that," said Cathleen. "Only—"

"Or you might marry some nice old widower with a couple of motherless children. You look quite alluring these days."

"I nearly did once. At Cabbage Tree. When you were about ten. Only—"

"Only what?"

"Only he was so ugly," said Cathleen. When Rosamund burst out laughing she rounded on her. "What's so funny?"

"Nothing. Just that you're so romantic. And it's all topsy-turvy. I'm the girl, you're the woman—yet I'm the practical one, and you're the romantic. Don't you see, mum, looks can't matter much in the long run. It's going the same way that matters, if you believe in the same things, have the same standards. Listen, skin only covers entrails, eyes are only jelly. Look at it like that and you'll bed down with Frankenstein's monster."

"Why don't you?" Cathleen snapped, not amused at all. I'm sick of waiting for people, she thought, sick of being told what to think. I'm sick of being lonely and frightened of being hurt. She stood up. "I'm going home to get on with my painting," she called over her shoulder. "I'm not waiting around any longer."

18

It was strange to Cathleen to find herself so restless. The rounded harmonies of sand-dunes and water, the tranquil stretch of bay with its bobbing craft at anchor, the mangroves endlessly, statically, observing their own reflections in the shallows were no longer a delight. Useless to remind herself of the subtle shifts from day to day, from season to season (from hour to hour, even.) Next week and next month and next year will be the same, always the same, she thought, looking through her windows to the placid prospect beyond. The horses will come down to the sands and pace out its perimeter, and swim with their unlikely heads out of the water, and be driven away. The jacarandas will lose their leaves in August and flower purple in November. And sometimes it will be a grey Swedish day, and sometimes a molten Mediterranean one, and sometimes just plain parti-coloured Australian, blue with milling clouds. But whatever the colour, it will be the same, always the same. And whether I step outside under the grape-vine, or watch behind glass, it will be the same for me. Because indoors or out, I am always behind glass, like dried flowers under a dome in a Victorian drawing-room.

She flung out her hand. Behind her the rosewood table teetered, tottered, fell. This way and that went old Mrs. Llewellyn's glass dome, all splintered, and the dried flowers crumbled to dust as they fell. Cathleen stood still, panicking for a moment as she always did at destruction or violence, or even suddenness. Then she swooped down, herself violent, and snatched up the pieces. A long sliver cut her fingers, and she laughed to see the blood.

"That's good!" she said, under her breath, and she dragged out a paper bag from the stock so thriftily disposed, so Alice-sit-by-the-fire. "I am forty years of age," she said to the brown-skinned woman in the bathroom mirror. Blood dripped—streamed—from her fingers. Not an artery, however, or it would be spurting. The antiseptic in the water was red, ruby-red. All these years that pallid blood, and now it is as red as a rose—no, as red as blood, she amended. As red as blood should be, and mine is, at last. Red as rubies, red as roses, red as heart's blood. Red, in fact, as life itself. And in no way from now on am I to be on the outside looking in. No way am I to live through my daughter. No way, in fact, to be cheated.

Caution, however, prevailed; and she sealed her life-blood inside (where, after all, it should be) with sticking-plaster, then with lint. Habit prevailed, and she rinsed out the basin, ran a comb through her hair. Alluring, Rosamund had said. Jokingly? Derisively? Or truly? Red warmed the silky skin that clothed her cheekbones, belied the sprinkle of grey in her nut-brown thatch. Brook-brown in their white circumference her eyes stared back at her. Startled, disarranged by her own gaze, she turned abruptly from the glass. Today should be my ironing day, she reminded herself, with the sheets all fresh and sun-smelling again after last week's deluge. Once it was my pleasure—pleasure—to fold and to iron, to stack all the neat arrays in linen press or wardrobe drawers. I stood back and smiled with pleasure, like God at the creation, she remembered, in disbelief. No wonder Rosamund mocked me.

Her fingers hurt as she pushed her way through the fly-screen. "Billy!" she called. "Bess!"

Bess came leaping; at twelve, absurdly, she was still limber. Billy followed more slowly.

"Anno domini, Billy," she whispered, bending to cup his little chin. "You and I both, darling. But there's still time left."

Even my walks have been channelled, she thought, hedged off for no reason at all, or for reasons long superseded. Once Billy had fought with the old foxie in Beach road—but it's years since those people moved away. The Alsatian in Campbell Street used to pick on Bess—but he died long ago. So if I want to climb up the hill to Faggotter's beach, or go down the avenue into the gully, there's nothing to stop me. But today, she said with resolution, I must break new ground, go somewhere I have never been before. Before they start cutting up the acres where the old dairy used to be, where the land fell into the sea, and people fear to build, before the bulldozers move into the wild side of the hill I must go there. Before it is too late. Billy is an old dog, he picks no fights, and for Bess I can take the leash. As she pushed back the gate the wattle, springing new after the rains, hit her in the face. She shivered in the air that gave warning of autumn, felt perverse pleasure in the cold that

154

goose-fleshed her arms. Have I awakened from long sleep, she wondered. Or from a spell? Or is it the red running in my veins that makes me want to run amok, face tigers—Or at least refuse to go back for a cardigan.

Children she had taught once peered out from their houses and waved to her. The Sampson boys, the Sullivans. Gap-toothed, stringy six year olds were shock-haired young lairs with beards, loading surfboards on dinted cars. The little girls of ten years back were pregnant: happy grotesques in Indian smocks with toddlers at their knees.

Her steps quickened. All these years I've lived here, and I've stayed on the tame side of the hill. Past the home-unit belt now, past the proliferation of widows, of old gentlemen retired from combat, except for their twice-a-week game of bowls. She was panting now, less from exertion than from the nearness of her escape. In ten years I'd be like them. Like the dried flowers crumbling to dust.

"Hi, Mrs. Bell," called a cheeky voice from the branches over her head, where John Seville perched precariously outside his tree-house. The wide-spaced eyes, so light and strange in his dark face, blinked into hers, and his wide mouth, crowded with about a hundred white teeth, laughed at her surprise. In a moment he had twisted upside-down, and was hanging by his knees, showing off.

"Hello, Johnny." Be careful, she wanted to say, and bit the words back. "That looks a good tree-house. Hang on tight, won't you?"

"Where are you going? Can I come too?" he called to her over and over again, till the wind carried his voice away. At the end of the road she turned and waved goodbye to him before she started the long climb upwards through the lantana and burrawong, over the tangle of fallen angophora branches and morning glory.

It was the hardest climbing she had ever done. So where am I going now, she asked herself, when she stood spent at the top of the hill and looked down to the unwelcoming, almost impenetrable bush beneath her. The slope before her feet was forbidding, even treacherous. She heard from a distance the sound of the sea crashing on rocks, but there was no glimpse of breakers, nor of sand. Casuarinas formed a thicket, not lacy, not filtering the sun as they did in the bay before her house, but dark and thick-set, blotting out what surely must be water beyond and below them. Somewhere near here, long ago, years ago, a great mass of the farm had fallen into the sea. Or so the tale went. She had lost all sense of direction, all sense of time.

Unleashed, Bess ran ahead. Billy walked close to her ankles, scratched from lantana. "Should we go back, old boy?" she asked him. "Or shall we go on to that angophora?"

Beside the grove of casuarinas stood one angophora, alone; dead, but it wouldn't lie down. Its long arms had taken the brunt of the winds that had whipped it bare: it stood now as survivor from seasons long past. Once it had presided over the farm that the old man had spoken of in his windy yarns. One of his fables, maybe, who could ever have farmed this harsh slope? And if it were true, it was all in the dreamtime, the pastures were overgrown and given back to the bush. So in the long run, Nature will triumph over man-made impediments, thought Cathleen; and this one tree which guarded or presided once, still stands. If Rosamund were here she would say that I am talking crap, that trees grow and die, not preside. But at least they do abide. The white ants come and make their strange habitations in the dead wood, and the kookaburras, opportunists, come to nest in them. Cathleen smiled with pleasure to see the baby birds, the tender grey of their feathers, their wobbly flights. On the roof of the world, on a dead branch piercing the dome above her, six kookaburras launched into their parody of song. Beneath her feet a dragon stirred, no, a lizard, flicking its blue tongue in and out as it faced the dogs.

Bess moved in, a black huntress. Cathleen aimed a kick at her. "Leave it alone!" Bess waited, tense. With infinite slowness the lizard slid beneath a log.

Billy was panting: he had had enough. No more, said his eyes, his almost-cataracted old eyes. No more, my mistress.

"Oh, alright, Billy," she said crossly. "But we'd better collar that hare-brained Bess." She whistled softly, then more loudly. Oh bugger it, she thought, using Rosamund's idiom. But I can't go home without her, for sure there'd be snakes in there.

She hesitated. A thread of track caught her eyes; it led under the biggest banksia she had ever seen, laden with black malevolent seed-pods, the bad banksia men of the children's

156

story. Regarded by their evil eyes she pushed on. A flower from the banksia tree brushed against her cheek as she stooped beneath a branch, and she broke it off, creamy, fluffy, quite firm against her cheek. I think it is my favourite tree, she thought, my very favourite. Oh mamma, not *another* favourite, she heard Rosamund's husky mocking voice at the back of her mind.

Quite close, almost directly behind the grove of casuarinas there was an explosion of barks. Of barks, of hisses, of crackling. Running now, Cathleen pushed under the last branches and leapt into a clearing. Over the long grass tumbled a strange animal, half-dog, half-cat. Now the cat pulled free and streaked away.

"Bess! Come here!" Into the bushes they ran, then back, and Billy, young again, took off in pursuit. If they catch it they mean to kill it, she realized helplessly, and dragged at the undergrowth for a stick that would achieve nothing. A squirt of water might stop them, but—the stick came loose, she swivelled to do her best with it, her useless best. But it was over. There was nothing to do. The cat, miraculously, was safe in a fallen log; and the dogs, atavistic but foiled, were barking and running in circles. Cathleen grabbed the leash and yoked them together, and drove them forward down the hill like oxen, until they were too far away to pounce again.

But the cat—could it get out? The thought of a cat, wedged tight through its own impetus, slowly starving to death was not to be contemplated. Yet how to get it out? How even to know whether in fact it was imprisoned there, or merely skulking. Perhaps it would have to be chopped free, or sawn free.

She knelt down. "Cat," she called, peering into the depths of the log. Slaters, a horde of them, poured out on to her hands. Blood seeped, then ran beneath the bandage. "Cat, are you lying doggo?"

Behind her a twig snapped. Above her a voice spoke. "Nymph, in thy orisons—"

Cathleen looked up. Burly he stood, as weathered as a tree, creases of laughter deepening about his blue eyes.

"Is it your cat?" she asked, still on her knees, and absurdly unable to rise. She felt quite weak, as if her insides had suddenly turned to jelly.

"It is." He moved a step closer. "And that, I take it, or those, are your dogs."

Cathleen took a breath. She tried again to stand, but could not. He put out his hands and lifted her to her feet, as easily as if she were made of paper.

"If Tom isn't out for tea, then I shall have to prise him out," he said. "Do you usually drive your animals like a pair of oxen?"

Cathleen bent to release them. They ran to sniff at the log, hopeful of more sport.

"There are half a dozen more cats dispersed around," said the after-all not quite god-like stranger. Taller than common men, and deeper-voiced, but not quite god-like. O brave new world, she thought, while she stood before him with eyes cast down. He spoke on. "With luck they may light upon a few more to chase up trees or down snake-holes, while you take tea with me."

Cathleen let him take her hand. Blood dripped onto his palm.

"What good red blood, madame," he remarked, respectfully.

Cathleen found her voice. "It wasn't once. It was pale once. I never had the energy to go for long walks."

"So that's why I never saw you before. For of course I should remember."

This is the web that Brian caught me in, thought Cathleen helplessly, in the web of words that binds you hand and foot. He is a practised womaniser—he has never been thwarted. "Is your wife at home?" she asked, boldly, gauchely.

"Wife I have none. Not now, anyway. But in the past I have had two or three." He was frankly laughing at her. "Not wife nor child, unless you count two strapping young men who go by someone else's name. Do you count them? No? It's a wise child that knows its own father." Was he joking? Cathleen could not tell, but when he smiled down at her, she hardly cared. "No, I live alone, except for my cats. And, of course, my objects."

Gazing around her, too bemused to observe decorum, Cathleen saw that she was indeed surrounded by objects. Stone ones and wooden ones, some just-begun, half-finished, finished, toppled over and discarded. Abstracts and spitting images. Huge and minuscule.

"You're a sculptor," she said idiotically.

"And you're a nymph." He stopped before a house as old as her own, and as ramshackle. Did it support the pittosporum that engulfed it, or the other way round? They were so intertwined that they would stand or fall together. Black with sump oil, as black as hers was white, his house was still unmistakably of the same vintage.

The door stood open. Within there was space, an old dresser, a scrubbed table. The design, the ground plan of the house was a replica of her own.

Cathleen smiled with pure joy. "It's like coming home. Ithaca. Your house is almost the twin of mine. I live in an old house down by the bay," she explained to his lifted brows.

"Alone?"

"With my daughter. When she is home, that is. On holidays. And sometimes at weekends."

"Ah!" He found this pleasing. He pumped up the primus and put on the kettle. "There's no electricity here."

"And you live like a noble savage. Was this once a farmhouse?" Over her first panicky shyness now, she felt very happy and easy. She sat in the chair he set for her and held out her hand obediently for his ministrations.

"Yes, to the second question. No to the first. Very mundane, my life. Not noble. What do you do when your child's away?"

"Well, nothing much. I teach little children for a living, and I look after my garden. I play the piano."

She searched her mind for some ploy he would find fascinating, and found instead his name. She jumped up. "You're Harry Donovan, aren't you? I heard you lived somewhere in exile."

"Voluntary exile." With fingers deft, although broad and blunted, he bandaged her hand and held it firmly. "I come out from time to time and make enough money to keep me going. But more and more I come out less and less. I've had my fill of Europe. And Sydney is bad now, too many people, too much high rise. I like to go into my fastness and close my doors against the world."

While he made the tea Cathleen stepped to the door and gazed outside. "I want to pinch myself awake. It's like the garden at Bomarzo. All those monsters."

"Thank you." He gave her tea in a brown cup. "I'm honoured."

"I didn't mean they were monstrous. I mean it is so surprising to find them—like the monsters at Bomarzo—the way your sculptures inhabit the garden. In fact," said Cathleen, throwing caution to the winds, "I really thought O brave new world"— She faltered into silence.

He was silent too. They drank their tea. "Did you like the garden at Bomarzo? It is one of the happiest memories of my time in Italy. That, and the orange persimmons on the purple trees along the hillsides."

She shook her head. The hot tea scalded her tongue. "I haven't been anywhere. Only school. And my garden. Sometimes a concert, I love music. But I read about gardens all over the world, Spain and Wales and Italy, everywhere. And sometimes I dream about them."

"And your husband?"

"I haven't got a husband. I never did. It was just an episode in the days when episodes were disgraceful."

"That accounts for your untouched look."

"How strange that you should say that. My daughter made the same observation."

He put his cup on the table, and moved with deliberation to her side. He smelled of sun and sweat, a good smell. If he put his arms around her, she would embrace him. Without question, without volition.

A wild yowling split the air. They sprang apart. Up two trees streaked two cats. Billy, supple as a pup, hurled himself at one of the trees, almost climbed it before he fell, and frenzied, tried again. Bess, more prudent, circled around.

The moment was shattered. "Your garden is beautiful," Cathleen said, composing her voice. She searched for something to say. "Is it true that the cowshed fell into the sea?"

"So I am told." He looked very cross; his face said that he took a dim view of being foiled.

Cathleen was unsure of herself. If she waited, silent, would he think her dull? If she spoke, would he think her a chatterbox? Quite distrait, she broke the silence. "That oak tree looks strange in this Australian landscape."

He stopped looking cross. "Yes, it does. The old couple planted it. It must be nearly a hundred years old. They planted forget-me-nots, too, and violets. And the woodbine. They were homesick for England, I suppose."

"And musk roses, of course!" she exclaimed in delight. A bank of them festooned the shed, pink ones with grey-green leaves. "Oh, how lovely!"

"I see that I shall have to marry you," he said, bantering, but—perhaps?—meaning it. "A lady dropped from the clouds who approves of my mode of life and knows her Shakespeare. After all it's ten years since I took a wife, and it's high time for me to beget children."

Cathleen felt a wave of desolation so strong that it was pain. "I think I've left it a bit late," she said abruptly. "I have to go now."

"I had hoped that you might stay the night with me," he said sociably. "But I expect your little daughter is waiting for you."

Big daughter, said Cathleen silently. Daughter of marriageable age. Oh, how unfair it is that men are young at forty, and women on the wane. She forced herself to smile, and spoke with false brightness. "I have promised myself to be there when the moonflowers open—and the white butterflies," she added senselessly.

"You know I have never seen moonflowers. Everything in the world, from lilacs to paw-paws, grows rampant in this garden, as I shall show you—as I shall have pleasure in showing you— but I have never seen a moonflower."

Cathleen was moving away from him. This is the man I have waited for, she knew in her bones, in her new-sprung blood. And I am too old for him. Am I? How old do you think I am, she wanted to ask. Did you mean what you said about children? Is forty too late? Mongol children, though, the little girl in my class with the mother of forty something.

"What fat magpies you have here," she said, by way of goodbye. Time, she must have time to think. "They seem almost domestic, not menacing, like Clifton Pugh's."

"Oh, Clifton! Do you know him?"

"No, just his work. My daughter is—is interested in art." Be careful, she admonished herself: maintain the fiction that your daughter is a child. Does love make you prevaricate, then?

161

Smitten, do you push truth down and hold it under?

"Good child. Very sound of her. All good for business." He watched her go. "Like the swan in the evening," he said gently as Cathleen moved away from him. At the edge of the clearing, where the swamp-irises thrust up their red spears, he called to her. "What is your name?"

"Cathleen."

"Cathleen," he repeated, narrowing his eyes in amusement and flattery, as he must have done again and again to scores of women, poor fools like me. There was a musician, he had a waltz he used over and over, he swore to each woman in turn that he had written it for her alone.

Cathleen looked levelly at him, and took a pace back. "You are like George Gershwin," she said. "With that waltz he wrote especially for about a hundred idiotic women."

He knew the story; he laughed aloud. "I am very susceptible," he said, then made the sign of the cross. "But this time—"

There was truth in him. Are you honest, sculptor?

Is it a game? Is it for real? Forever even?

He seemed to read her thoughts. "I am at long last ready to settle with one woman. If she is as good as she is beautiful, and prepared to share my wilderness."

"Paradise," said Cathleen. "As well you know."

He nodded, sure of himself, very sure of his male strength. Irish, perhaps, with those dark lashes, and that blarneying tongue. Clancy, she thought, Donovan, I am their victuals.

"Perhaps you will bring me some moonflower seeds?" he asked. "By way of sealing our pact."

Cathleen nodded, in her turn. She dipped under the casuarinas into a dark and shaded world, ricketed over the fallen banksia pods, looked up into the branches of the great banksia, crowded with little ancient black heads, all chattering together. An hour ago she had come this way; or a lifetime. The dogs sniffed at the log where the lizard had taken shelter, but found nothing. An hour ago. She tasted it again, all the sweetness of a lifetime's waiting distilled into one hour; she touched it and tasted, and held it to the light, a hive of honey. Do I dare?

"I dare everything," she said aloud to her listeners, to the banksia men, to the cocked ears of the dogs, to her new-stocked pounding heart.

19

Cathleen came home before dusk to an empty house. She stood
outside in her garden and watched the moonflowers open: one
moment their white petals were clenched tight, and next they
were flaring open. Their scent was sweet and remote, a scent
that seemed to drift from a land and a time far away. I could go
back now, she thought, I could take the moonflowers and hold
them out to him, and he would draw me close. But if he found
me too bold, thought me a light woman, a night's pastime,—no,
I must wait. Perhaps he was only half in earnest, perhaps it was
all a dream, something I made up. If I wait one day, or two, I
can pretend that I was passing by. Surely I can wait two days.

All her new-found, hard-won essays into independence were
swamped in a wave of bliss so enveloping that it was euphoria.
She watched the boats that had put out that morning, turn
towards home, saw the first mists rise from the bushland on the
far shore. The first chill of autumn was in the air. She heard a
currawong pipe his cheeky call, come here boy, come here boy,
as she stood barefoot and silent, waiting for some sign that
would tell her something she needed to know, some signal that
would say go or stay. The moon rose, and she waited. The
moon on the water, the soft lap of the incoming tide made her
heart ache as it had not ached for twenty years. Wispy clouds,
stars dispersed and bright in a dark-blue sky, and I am mooning
like a green girl. I am moonstruck.

At the gate the dogs barked: Rosamund. In a flash Cathleen
was in her room, with the door shut. By the time the front door
had opened she had pulled off her dress, slid under the sheets in
her petticoat. When Rosamund called she did not answer. She
lay still and listened to the sounds in the kitchen, heard Billy
grumbling because he had been left outside, heard Rosamund
consoling him. The crack of light under the door was gone.
Rosamund's door opened and shut. The house lay quiet.

Cathleen lay quiet also, and heard the sound of her own
heart. She turned on her other side to escape it, buried her head
in the pillow; but it sounded like a tom-tom. She heard the
minutes tick away on the French ormolu clock on her bedside
table; a present from Rosamund last year; a million cherries she

had picked to pay for it. Or so she said.

At last Cathleen could bear it no longer. She threw back the sheets, swung her legs out of the bed, pulled on a kimono. Barefooted she tiptoed out on to the verandah, and put her arms around the great jacaranda that had grown from the seed she had planted. The bark scratched her cheek as she rubbed her face against it.

A board creaked, a door opened. It was Rosamund, robust in pyjamas. The moonlight touched her calm face, gilded further her tousled crown.

"Can't you sleep either? I didn't wake you when I came in, did I?"

Cathleen shook her head. "No. I think it must have been the cestrum, it's too potent, really. Or maybe it was the moonlight streaming through my window." She was hedging, keeping Rosamund at bay. "I'll have to move the cestrum away from the house, it muddles my sleep."

"Interferes, you mean."

"No, it muddles me. It smells like something in an enchanted garden, if you breathed in too deeply you'd be transported or lost—or something." Nothing in the world would make her speak of an encounter too sudden, words too seductive for alien ears. So my daughter is an alien, she realised with a shock: in this turning-point of my life she is alien and I am alone.

"Remember our bargain, old woman? You promised never to mention fairy-tales again." Rosamund's voice was serious and loving.

"Our bargain?"

"At Granada. When I said you were frozen in a dream, and life was for living. All that. And you promised."

How beautiful she is, my daughter. Well worth the twenty years gone into her shaping. But now it is time for me to live for myself, thought Cathleen.

"You were right," she answered. "I was clinging to the past because at least it was there. I was sure of it, and the future was so uncertain. There were lots of things you were right about," she said quickly, so that Rosamund with her antennae would not guess too much. "About lichens being beautiful, and eggs being a perfect shape—"

"Speaking of eggs," said Rosamund, side-tracked, "I took

164

that terrible yellow budgie's eggs away from her and smashed them. She's altogether too fertile, and it costs too much to feed them. But I agree, they look charming with their little blue noses buried in the bread, munching. I took the time to really look at them while I was cleaning out the aviary. Where were you?"

"Oh, nowhere really," said Cathleen, deliberately vague. "Walking—"

"Shall I make us a cup of coffee?"

"If you like."

"Shall I put on our pet counter-tenor? Mamma, come to earth! Do you want to hear Alfred?"

"No!" Cathleen's voice was sharp.

"As you please. But wouldn't you like to have a little weep when that gorgeous falsetto gets to work on the maestro's lyrics?"

"Rosamund, I said no. I'm not in the mood."

"Odd," retorted Rosamund as she went. "I'd have sworn that you were. One of his later records, then. Not so unearthly, but still—" She spoke from the other room, her voice muffled. "Maybe I'll take off next week, mamma. Later on I'll go to Scandinavia, I think. But in the meantime—well, as I think you know, I've finally stopped dreaming about Desportes and all his kind. I'm casing the field with a new vision. You're probably right, you know. The burly guys are probably better in the long run for a dame like me. I think I'll go back to Tasmania for the apple-picking. And I'll keep my eyes peeled for a good guy, and thank Heaven fasting for a good man's love, etcetera. And present you with a brace or two of grandchildren to cluck over, two plain, two coloured—adopted, don't flinch. And get on with my painting—There's so *much* I've got to crowd in!" she almost shouted.

Cathleen took the cup she was offered. She had flinched not at the thought of Rosamund's ideal family, which was after all a notion she had heard many times over, but at the assumption that the young were to do the living, and the middle-aged were to stand on the outskirts. Of course, she reminded herself, it was always like that. I was always background music. I carried the spears, and she starred. And now she has grown up, and we have survived, and learned to trust each other. So perhaps I

165

should tell her what I hardly know myself.

"I love you very much, mamma," said the girl who was adept at knowing the right moment. "Don't think that I won't be back, one way or another. We've taught each other a good bit, I reckon. You've tidied me up, and I've dishevelled you a bit. And of course I bullied you into getting yourself well again."

They fell silent. Stronger than the hot cestrum, but mingled with it, the angel's trumpet breathed out its cool yet musky smell. Those two plants, they smell like evil and innocence, thought Cathleen.

"Boy, does this garden pong!" said Rosamund, striding to the limits of the verandah and leaping off. She bent down and lifted up two snails, cupped in her hands. "See," she said, "Two young lovers, lately wed. Think of the thousands of lovely babies they'll have. Or shall I kill them now, at the very height of their transports?" Young and destructive, she weighed their fate; then put them under the willow. "If a bird gets them it's out of my hands. But for my part I intend to observe clemency." She put her hands up to the lower branches, swung up and out. "How it's grown. Remember when I was a kid I had a swing there."

"The borers have got to it," said Cathleen mournfully. "Its days are numbered."

"Well, put in some cuttings and start again." Rosamund hesitated. "So it looks as if I'll get going this week, mamma. But first I'll clean out the guttering for you, and chop up the winter firewood."

"I can do it myself now," said Cathleen aloud. And silently she added, perhaps I won't have to: perhaps I'll be somewhere else too. An exquisite expectation pierced her: perhaps I'll have better things to do than sit and wait.

Rosamund yawned. "I'm going to bed anyway. I hope I won't piss the bed after all that coffee and sentiment. Sorry, mum, I forgot I was speaking to a lady." She cleared the distance between them in one step, and planted a brusque kiss on Cathleen's scalp. "I'll leave you to your mooning. I'm buggered."

The moon had set and the stars were fading before she went back to bed. Behind the folds of hill he would be stirring, watching dawn streak the horizon, hearing the birds begin to chaffer. Or perhaps he would be sleeping still. No, she amended, he would get up with the dawn, as I must learn to do: his rhythms will be mine from this time on. She fell into a sleep, restless at first, then deep. While the sun gave warning of its intention she slept, while it rose dripping from the pearly chambers of the sea and soared triumphant, she slept on. At midday she woke to the cheerful sound of chopping, and the agreeable smell of coffee.

"Good morning," she called to the figure in brown corduroys, bent over a pile of wood. "Watch out for funnel-webs. You look like the nigger in the woodpile."

"Racist!" said Rosamund. "Yes, well I just disposed of an enormous one. Brutal, of course, but I couldn't be merciful. There's coffee in there, and pancakes, if you want them. I thought you'd been drugged or murdered, you looked as if you'd never wake up."

In the shower, Cathleen looked at herself. As she soaped her body, she saw that it was slender and agreeably made. The stretch-marks on her belly had faded to a pale silvery tracery that was not unattractive. Her round breasts, though not a girl's, were still firm-fleshed. She gazed dispassionately at the woman in the glass, and pondered. The swift steps on the verandah heralded Rosamund—with movements as swift as a girl's, Cathleen seized a towel and covered herself. When her daughter came in to wash her hands, Cathleen was drying her hair.

"You've got your programme to do today, haven't you? If you get it done early, I thought we might go for a tramp around the foreshores. It's low tide, I think? Or even right along the coastline to the lighthouse."

"What programme?" Cathleen had forgotten she had six weeks of lessons to be mapped out, the stories and poems to be chosen and recorded, the games, the formal work.

"Although I daresay you can do it on your ear now. Mum, I was thinking, now that you feel so much better you might want to try for promotion. Or at least not avoid it as you've done before. You might as well rise in the world." When Cathleen shook her head Rosamund tried again. "Alright then. Or learn to play the cello. Or you could join one of those Renaissance music groups, grab yourself a sackbut or a rebec or something, and get cracking. You've got all that brand-new energy to use up. Who knows, you might even get yourself a guy."

Cathleen's hands, twisting the towel into a turban over her wet hair, stopped; then went on twisting. "Don't worry about me, Rosamund," she said. "I'll survive."

It was the longest day that Cathleen could ever remember. Each hour stretched out interminably, as it does to a child before Christmas, to a woman before her baby is born. Perhaps time goes haywire for old people too, she thought: stretches out or telescopes. She remembered old Mr. Jackson pulling out oxalis from his lawn, with a patience and perseverance that seemed bizarre to the onlooker. And now he was dead, and his wife too, so the weeds grew unchecked in the unmown lawns, the annuals died, the shrubs drooped; and the house waited for some young couple to breathe life into it again.

Cathleen curled her bare toes languorously into soil as she listed singing games in her neat script in the neatly-ruled precisely-divided page before her. "Looby Loo", she wrote; "I had a little nut tree"; "Punchinello". She forced her gaze back from the turquoise berries on the vine, from the mandevilleas celebrating summer's end, rioting, in fact, along Rosamund's new fence. The page in front of her waited to be filled. "Red leaves, gold leaves" she wrote in the column reserved for songs. Autumn is coming, and the days grow colder. Rosamund will go; and so shall I.

In fact Rosamund had rehearsed her final leave-taking, gone tramping with the dogs somewhere along the jagged coastline where the blue-ringed octopus lies in the rock pools, and the cliffs rear high above. This day will never be done with, said Cathleen to herself, and put down her pen. Black or purple, the Isabella grapes dropped to the ground below, and lay there, globes all smashed, while the ants milled around them. She watched the colloquies, the immense burdens (one minute crumb) they bore away to their storerooms, like Egyptian slaves. Or the other way round: the toilers in the Pyramids came long after the ants. Bees, their wings frayed with summer's foraging, dug into the buddleia blossoms, their striped behinds upended and waggling. Summer never ripens until it is time to say goodbye; and we call it back, and it lingers for a moment, then is gone. With severity she called her wandering attention to the near-blank of the page that waited.

Each day, inescapably, must come to an end. Sun, in the end, comes to the rim of the world: the technicolour mishmash of sunset is over. Cathleen picked a paw-paw from the tree. How Rosamund had teased (Paw-paws here? In this olde-worlde garden? Poor show, ma!). How meekly she had bowed her head. Stupid really, the answer was plain: I grow them for you and your gluttonous friends. If you eat you should not scorn. But the quick retort had never been given; no wonder Rosamund had grown so powerful. Cathleen scooped seeds from the paw-paw, sliced it, and ate a fragment to quell the gnawing of a belly empty but not inclined for food.

Day lingered. Birds sought their nests. Soon the owls would come out in the park, and swoop on their prey. Poor mice: one creature's meat is another's doom. The way of nature is cruel, although pared-down and necessary. To prey is necessary, thought Cathleen Bell, watching the fisherman hold a flapping fish silhouetted against the sky.

She turned to go inside. Still no Rosamund. A little uneasy, she turned her anxiety into crossness. The dogs would be hungry, it was too bad that she was keeping them out. She frowned; sighed with relief as she heard the gate click. With a bound onto the protesting boards, Rosamund resumed residence. Her mass of hair had come loose from its plait, her legs were scratched, her dress ripped.

"I went to the wild side of the hill, mum!" she said. "The dogs found their way into a fantastic garden there. A guy lives there all by himself."

"Yes, I know," said Cathleen after a moment. "A sculptor, isn't he? Quite a celebrated one." She turned away, guarding her secret. "I've cut up a paw-paw."

"Great!" cried Rosamund. "But I stink like a pole-cat, whatever that is. I guess I'd better have a shower." She whisked away.

Cathleen opened two cans of dog food for her starving hounds, who were patrolling the doors to remind her of her negligence. They were covered in cobbler's pegs, and Billy had dried blood across his nose. "I suppose you're alive with ticks," she said, fondling his ears. Tomorrow would do to go over them. Tomorrow was for everything. Tomorrow after school I

169

shall go up the hill with my moonflower seeds, she decided suddenly, nothing will stop me. I've waited long enough, too long. And if he asks me to stay, I will. And if it lasts a day or a year, I don't care, I am done with my glass case.

"Rosamund," she called to the bathroom door, freshly painted by the now-splashing occupant. "I'm going to bed. I'm tired out. I didn't sleep much."

"Wait on. I'll be right out."

Cathleen was gone. She took off her clothes, pulled on her nightgown; tomorrow perhaps she would sleep naked. She shivered. Absurd to feel so shy, why the fourteen years olds are adept at the love game now, they tell me, or at least they know the tricks of the trade. So Rosamund says, the big O she calls it. But you wouldn't know about that, my innocent little mamma.

At the door Rosamund was tapping, firmly at first, then tentatively.

"Please don't come in, darling," whispered Cathleen, her voice furry with deceit. "I'm almost asleep. But if I start talking I'll be awake all night."

"Oh alright, old woman!" said the wide-awake voice. "I'll let you off in view of your advanced years."

Did Cathleen sleep? Sometimes. Sometimes she tossed and dreamed. In her dreams a lion roared and moved towards her, then lay down at her feet like a cat. "Oh, what a lovely cat!" all the people surrounding cried out in admiration. "Please give me a kitten!" begged a little girl. "When he has kittens, please—" Cathleen woke with tears in her eyes, but tears of happiness. It makes no more sense than this dream—all that has happened, all that I hope—and yet I must hope, and yet I do believe. When he sees me again he will know how stupid I am, and that will be the end of it, I suppose.

Nevertheless at first light she rose and went to the moonflower vine. At first she could find only green pods, then at last a ripe one, and another. One for sorrow, two for joy: two would be enough.

"What are you doing up so early?" called Mr. McKenzie on his way past, squinting at her.

"I couldn't sleep." She pulled her nightgown across her chest.

"Neither could I. My arthritis was playing up Old Harry!" He was disposed to linger.

Harry? Why did he say old Harry. Just a phrase, she reminded herself, and sketched a smile of goodbye as she took her seeds inside. Half past six—half past five really. Daylight saving would be ending soon. She put the seeds on the table, next to a rag soaked in turps that Rosamund had thrown there. She had been painting in the night then, thought Cathleen, with relief: criminal to have a talent like hers and discard it. Still too impatient to learn her craft methodically, she came to it by fits and starts, learning by trial and error, as Brian had done.

From her tidy larder Cathleen took a jar of cumquat marmalade, neatly labelled, sealed with care. No wonder Rosamund had laughed at her, everything so tidily in place. She was starving, she discovered. She carried her coffee and toast to the seat beneath the trellis and ate hungrily. Let the dogs wait for once. Too restless to sit, she carried it back inside.

The flushing of the cistern proclaimed Rosamund's entry on the day's round. Splendidly regular in all her rhythms, unashamedly proud of her body as a going concern. It would take a pretty good man to cut her down to size, a hero, really. Desportes had said she was like an egg: man, woman and child all in one. Now she swung out of the bathroom, hair too yellow, eyes too blue. Only God and God alone—how did the poem go? For once memory was inadequate.

"Mum," said Rosamund, without preamble. "I wasn't going to tell you, but I think I should. Because after all you were the one who got me into it."

"Into what?" Cathleen was packing her brief case.

"Well, you know how you always said I'd be better with a real man instead of the sods I got hold of. Even if he clouted me—"

Embedded in the cheekiness of her voice was a quiver. Cathleen listened, frozen now, but for no good reason.

"Well, I told you. On the other side of the hill—"

The silence between them was filled with sound.

"Well?" asked Cathleen, gripping the table, her knuckles white.

"I met this man there. It was—cataclysmic."

"And he—how did he feel?" She waited, with sinking heart.

"He liked me, I think. He said I was beautiful. He said my name was beautiful, rose of the world. He was wary. But I think he had a letch for me."

171

Be quiet, Cathleen wanted to shout. Letch, stuff, screw. What do you know of love, you children? "How do you know? Did he ask you to stay with him?"

Rosamund shook her head. She gave a gulp before she spoke. "No. But he will—I'm so much younger—and I admire him so much, admire his work, well that's him really. We're both so independent—oh, can't you see how right it is—" She looked at Cathleen for reassurance. "Do you really think I'm pretty?"

Cruel girl. All the world filled with men to fall at your feet, and this one, it has to be this one—With great sadness Cathleen saw her daughter as vulnerable, not armoured at all; saw that she was needed now for this last gift of love.

"Beautiful," said Cathleen, with stiff lips. "Not pretty, beautiful. And he couldn't fail to love you."

Rosamund took a deep breath. "You're never wrong," she said exultantly. "So I'll get going. No sense in hanging around. Don't worry if I'm not home tonight. I'll be alright."

What about me, Cathleen wanted to ask. What am I to do? The king has killed his heart, she thought, incoherent with pain.

But Rosamund's face was shining with love and gratitude. She opened her palms for the moonflower seeds that Cathleen thrust at her.

"You can take these," said Cathleen. "They're the only thing he hasn't got in his garden."

Love had made Rosamund blind and deaf and senseless; she found no nuance in Cathleen's words, hardly apprehended them. She wrapped the seeds in a wad of turps-soaked rag.

"Oh, you know the garden?" She turned to go, clutching them in her fist, young, strong and invincible.

"You'll kill them," said Cathleen. "Holding them so tight."

"Never mind. Plenty more where they came from." The gate swung open.

It should be my heart in a casket she is taking, thought Cathleen, bleakly, holding on to the verandah post for support.

The dogs gambolled, traitors, came bounding to the girl's whistle.

"Leave me my dogs," called Cathleen, running down the steps. "Billy, Bess. Come back!" No use. The wind brought her voice back to her.

The wall of wattle parted to let them through, girl and

172

hounds: closed behind them. Cathleen leaned against the paper-barks she had planted so long ago; and the bells that Rosamund had hung along the branches swung this way, that way, sounded their sweet and tatty chimes.

THE RUNNING YEARS

Claire Rayner

She was born in 1893, in the slums of London. The daughter of immigrants, the descendants of exiles, she was part of a people doomed to wander, forever strangers in the lands they had chosen as home.

But Hannah Lazar was different. She was born and bred a Londoner, and London was where she belonged. As Strong-willed as she was beautiful, Hannah would uproot herself from the gloomy poverty of her parents' lives to enter a world of elegance and wealth. As her ancestors had journeyed from land to land, with only their own resilience and determination to help them survive, Hannah would move from the slums of the East End to the salons of Mayfair, to a life that she could call her own.

The Running Years is Claire Rayner's most powerful and spectacular novel to date, a breathtaking testament to the human spirit – a richly dramatic and intricately woven story that traces the fortunes of two Jewish families from the razing of Jerusalem in 70 AD through two thousand years of violence, love and change.

'A huge canvas, this, with powerful characters and a gripping story' *Woman's own*

'A feast' *Yorkshire Post*

BESTSELLING FICTION FROM ARROW

All these books are available from your bookshop or news-agent or you can order them direct. Just tick the titles you want and complete the form below.

☐	THE COMPANY OF SAINTS	Evelyn Anthony	£1.95
☐	HESTER DARK	Emma Blair	£1.95
☐	1985	Anthony Burgess	£1.75
☐	2001: A SPACE ODYSSEY	Arthur C. Clarke	£1.75
☐	NILE	Laurie Devine	£2.75
☐	THE BILLION DOLLAR KILLING	Paul Erdman	£1.75
☐	THE YEAR OF THE FRENCH	Thomas Flanagan	£2.50
☐	LISA LOGAN	Marie Joseph	£1.95
☐	SCORPION	Andrew Kaplan	£2.50
☐	SUCCESS TO THE BRAVE	Alexander Kent	£1.95
☐	STRUMPET CITY	James Plunkett	£2.95
☐	FAMILY CHORUS	Claire Rayner	£2.50
☐	BADGE OF GLORY	Douglas Reeman	£1.95
☐	THE KILLING DOLL	Ruth Rendell	£1.95
☐	SCENT OF FEAR	Margaret Yorke	£1.75

Postage _____

Total _____

ARROW BOOKS, BOOKSERVICE BY POST, PO BOX 29, DOUGLAS, ISLE OF MAN, BRITISH ISLES

Please enclose a cheque or postal order made out to Arrow Books Limited for the amount due including 15p per book for postage and packing both for orders within the UK and for overseas orders.

Please print clearly

NAME..

ADDRESS..

....

Whilst every effort is made to keep prices down and to keep popular books in print, Arrow Books cannot guarantee that prices will be the same as those advertised here or that the books will be available.